Death at 24 Elliot Street

Tom Wall

Death at 24 Elliot Street

Olympia Publishers
London

www.olympiapublishers.com
OLYMPIA PAPERBACK EDITION

Copyright © Tom Wall 2025

The right of Tom Wall to be identified as author of
this work has been asserted in accordance with sections 77 and 78 of
the Copyright, Designs and Patents Act 1988.

All Rights Reserved

No reproduction, copy or transmission of this publication
may be made without written permission.
No paragraph of this publication may be reproduced,
copied or transmitted save with the written permission of the publisher,
or in accordance with the provisions
of the Copyright Act 1956 (as amended).

Any person who commits any unauthorised act in relation to
this publication may be liable to criminal
prosecution and civil claims for damage.

A CIP catalogue record for this title is
available from the British Library.

ISBN: 978-1-83543-836-7

This is a work of fiction.
Names, characters, places and incidents originate from the writer's
imagination. Any resemblance to actual persons, living or dead, is
purely coincidental.

First Published in 2025

Olympia Publishers
Tallis House
2 Tallis Street
London
EC4Y 0AB

Printed in Great Britain

Dedication

I dedicate this book to my darling wife, Diane.

Acknowledgments

Known in the music industry as the man who signed U2 to their first record contract, Jackie Hayden has published over twenty-five books, either under his own name or as a ghost writer/editor. My very special thanks to Jackie for his early help and support with developing my manuscript. Jackie comes from Dublin and lives in County Wexford.

My grateful thanks to Gilly Withers, classics scholar and teacher who was the first to opine with encouragement on my manuscript.

Chapter 1

For two ordinary ladies, the day started like any normal working day. But it would not remain normal for long.

On that fateful Monday, Mrs Ivy drove her cherished Mini to collect her assistant Molly Parks at eight-thirty a.m. from her house in Durnford Street, Plymouth. Peggy Ivy was older than Molly, who was a single mum living with her mother and baby boy. Peggy's husband was aboard a Royal Navy ship somewhere between Plymouth and Singapore.

The two women worked well together, getting on with their cleaning while chatting about life in Plymouth, the latest scandals and speculating as to whether Tom Jones was really going to appear at the Theatre Royal the following month.

Fifty-eight years old, Peggy Ivy was a dab hand at cleaning and worked a number of the buildings near Plymouth Hoe. The "dream team", as they liked to call themselves, usually started at the apartments at the Grand where Peggy was allowed to park her car in the underground car park. They were responsible for cleaning the stairways and the Gladstone Room, which used to be the waiting room and communal lounge in the former hotel.

Peggy had a separate agreement to clean the developer Charles Bartlett's apartment, number nineteen on the third floor. Bartlett didn't own the apartment, but as the developer, he was allowed to use it as his base when in Plymouth. Peggy was trusted with the key to number nineteen and kept it locked safely in a box at home when she was not using it.

After collecting their vacuum cleaner from where it was stored in a cupboard in the Gladstone Room, Molly carried their two buckets with their favourite sprays and cloths, stepping aside to allow Peggy to open the door to number nineteen. On venturing inside, Peggy was taken aback to find Charles Bartlett slumped over the dining table. At first sight she and Molly assumed he was asleep, especially as there was nothing askew in the room. But, as they approached the still figure, they suspected something was wrong. Despite the noise of their arrival, Mr Bartlett had not moved.

On the verge of panic, Peggy promptly called the managing agent's office, suggesting that Mr Bartlett might have suffered a heart attack. Before long an ambulance arrived, and it only took a cursory examination at the scene before the paramedics declared him dead. They promptly reported their findings back to their base, who immediately sent a doctor to confirm the diagnosis.

Mr Charles Bartlett was indeed dead. The doctor in turn alerted the police, as was required in such instances. Devon and Cornwall Constabulary soon arrived on the scene and immediately sealed off the apartment pending the arrival of a detective.

As Peggy Ivy explained to them, the door had been locked from the inside by the simple act of turning a short chrome lever. There was no indication of a break-in. A half-empty glass of wine stood on the table, its contents probably having been poured from a bottle also on the table. The cork also lay close by, still skewered into a corkscrew, and the lead foil cover from the bottle lay alongside. The police took all the items away for analysis as a matter of course, including two unopened bottles in the wine cooler.

Some two years earlier, Jack and Penny Sinnott had driven down from London and parked nearby at the entrance to the Esplanade in front of Plymouth Hoe. The purpose of their trip was an appointment to visit an apartment property with a local estate agent, Ann Barton. The property had been advertised as offering stunning sea views and generously spaced rooms.

On inspection, Jack formed the view that it seemed tired and in need of about £100,000 to be spent on it before it would make the grade. Penny was equally unenthusiastic, and after a quiet chat, they thanked Ann for showing them around but said it was not quite what they were looking for.

They were about to head back home when Ann suggested that they might be interested in an apartment across the street in the Grand and offered to take them to the first-floor apartment, number five.

As Ann explained, the Grand was still under refurbishment from the devastating effects of a fire, and the building's halcyon days as a hotel were over. A developer, with backing from a commercial bank, was in the process of refurbishing the building into twenty-six luxury apartments, a challenging task in itself, given the building's Grade II listed status and the stringent demands of Plymouth Council Planning that he must retain the elegance of the original Victorian building.

Penny was very familiar with Plymouth, a city she loved. She was born there to William "Bill" Henry Parsons and his wife Doris. Bill's parents had died when he was young, and he was reared by his aunt. His father had been a sea captain, and Bill took to the sea like a duck to water. He was brought up in the Barbican area of Plymouth and attended navigation classes at Mannamead College (later known as Plymouth College), and over time, graduated as an Admiralty Pilot. Prior to his retirement in 1983, he had worked as the Plymouth Sound pilot. He had also worked in Royal Navy dockyards around the world, including Malta, Gibraltar, Singapore and Portsmouth, to mention only a few.

So, while it was easy to understand Penny's connection to both the sea and her birthplace, Jack was a "blow-in" from Ireland to the UK where he had long happily settled.

As the estate agent showed them around, he immediately became fascinated by the history of the building and was drawn to the blue plaque on the wall by the front door. It formally stated that in 1889, William Ewart Gladstone, MP, and former Prime Minister, aged eighty-one, spoke from the first-floor balcony of the Grand Hotel on Plymouth Hoe. The assembled audience was reported to be ten-thousand strong. He was trying to advance the case for Home Rule for Ireland, euphemistically referred in Britain as "The Irish Problem". Jack had learnt to bite his tongue at such references, as he knew that the real problem was the English King George IV. The King later gave his endorsement to the Home Rule Bill following persuasion from the Irishman Arthur Wellesley, better known as the Duke of Wellington. Sadly, the First World War intervened, and the Act was never put into effect.

Ms Barton also highlighted the significant features of the area around the building, citing the fact that Lady Astor, MP for Plymouth lived in number three Elliot Terrace, the same building they had just viewed across the street from the Grand. 'As you may know,' she said, 'she was the first female MP.' Jack bit his tongue again and hesitated to correct her, knowing that Astor, who was the daughter of a wealthy tobacco farmer in Virginia, may indeed have been the first lady MP to take her seat in the House of Commons. But the Irish woman, Lady Markievicz, was the first elected female MP. Like all those who fought for Irish independence, she did not take her seat in Westminster.

The apartment included an orangery, an attractive enclosed space with four large sash windows offering views across Plymouth Sound. It was reputed to be the one of the best in Europe but Jack thought it had to be one of the best in the world. The ceilings were so high that an unfinished stairway led to a mezzanine gallery large enough for a platoon of marines.

Jack climbed a ladder to view the floor complete with a utility room, separate bathroom and cupboards. Two additional bedrooms had en-suite facilities below. In addition, each apartment was allocated a parking space underground. He knew straight away that if they were to have an apartment in Plymouth, this was the one. So, after comparatively little consideration, they bought it and moved in during December 2010.

The financial crisis had already hit two years earlier but had only now begun to bite in Devon, and the ensuing decline in property sales meant that initially only a few of the twenty-six apartments were occupied. Little did Jack know then, but the financial downturn would turn out to have a more serious impact on his life than he might ever have suspected.

Chapter 2

Sinnott is a family name only rarely heard in Plymouth, but the Sinnott clan have long-established roots in the south-east of Ireland, and the name is prominent in County Wexford. They not only made their contribution to Irish independence but also served abroad with distinction in the Crown Forces, as did thousands of Irishmen. Sir Walter Scott Sinnott, son of the noble family of Sinnott of Somersetshire, came to Ireland with Richard de Clare, better known as Strongbow, in the year 1170 as part of the Anglo-Norman occupation of Ireland during the reign of Henry II. Sinnott was granted lands formerly owned by the Mac Murraghs.

Lance Corporal John Sinnott (1829-1896) was an Irish recipient of the Victoria Cross for his conspicuous gallantry at India's northern city of Lucknow in October 1857. The Siege of Lucknow (May – November, 1857) was a sustained assault that brought the eventual relief of the British "Residency" (British governmental headquarters) as part of the Indian Mutiny against British rule.

In the Cromwellian years in Ireland, David Sinnott was governor of Wexford town. He tried to negotiate a peace treaty with Oliver Cromwell to spare the town from a massacre as horrific as that experienced by the innocent citizens in Drogheda also under savage Cromwell's orders. It is said that even as Sinnott and he met, Cromwell's cannons were already pounding the walls of Wexford town. These were not Cromwell's finest hours, especially given that he is reported to have considered himself a God-fearing, honourable man.

As matters turned out, the Sinnotts soon lost their land in County Wexford, but the life of at least one of their descendants was to become entwined with that of Britain in unexpected ways centuries later.

Jack Sinnott had been a rather lazy, dreamy student at St Peter's College at Summerhill in his hometown of Wexford, the capital of the county. A secondary school for boys, St Peter's was founded in 1811, initially as a seminary to prepare students for the Catholic priesthood. The college moved to the impressive Pugin-designed building around 1819.

In his penultimate year at St Peter's, Jack developed a love for English prose and poetry and history. He would often muse over the irony of contrasting historical events happening at the same time in different places. Thus, his interest in the historic background to the Grand in Plymouth.

He was aware that during the summer of 1798, the poets William Wordsworth and Samuel Taylor Coleridge walked the Quantock Hills of Somerset, an experience of such depth that it inspired some of the most beautiful and most memorable poems in the history of mankind. Coleridge finished his blood-curdling ballad "The Rime of the Ancient Mariner", which he was inspired to write at Watchet Harbour on the coast of Somerset. There he had sat by the harbour wall, observing the comings and goings of the fishermen. He would have seen the bearded loons with their faces weathered over the years by wind and sun into a shiny brown, leather-like surface, as they sat puffing on their clay pipes, bemoaning the poor catch of the day.

Wordsworth was still working on the manuscript for Lyrical Ballads before he wrote *Lines Composed a Few Miles Above*

Tintern Abbey, pioneering a new trend for poetry highlighting the link between nature and man. These were all familiar poems to Jack Sinnott.

Ironically, in the same month and year, on the opposite side of the Irish Sea, one-hundred-twenty poorly armed but brave Irishmen, both Protestant and Catholic alike, lay hidden behind a ditch on Oulart Hill in County Wexford. From the high vantage point on a clear day, you can see the mountains of Leinster across the valley, and some even claimed you could also make out the hills of west Wales.

The Irish fighters were known as "Pikemen" because the weapon they mainly used in battle was a spear-like object attached to a long wooden pole. A curved hook off one side of the spear was designed to drag troopers off their horses.

On that day, the pikemen lay silent and motionless, steeling themselves for an imminent attack from the mounted cavalry of the North Cork Militia. The Corks, as they were known, were a military unit of Irishmen sponsored by the English Crown and stationed at Wexford Castle about twenty kilometres south of Oulart Hill.

Pat Sinnott, a wealthy farmer, was central in organising the Wexford men for the coming encounter. These were indeed hard times in Ireland, as they were in England, for the underprivileged and oppressed. But the imposition of penal laws governing land tenancy was the straw that broke the camel's proverbial across Ireland. The Corks assumed they were about to face a rabble of poorly armed and disorganised Irish rebels. So confident were they of an easy victory that their wives had asked them to bring back some souvenirs from Oulart.

As they advanced up the hill, the Corks spotted a section of the Irish, mostly women and children, running away from behind a ditch. They saw this as their opportunity to sort out the Wexford rebels once and for all, and their officer-in-charge gave the order to 'come to the trot' and 'draw sabres'.

Within two hundred yards of the ditch, the order was given to 'come into line'. This involved the troopers spreading out across the length of the ditch in preparation for charging forward. The bugler was ordered to sound the charge with the officer shouting, 'the line will attack.'

A cavalry charge is military drama personified. The players are the horses, their riders and the enemy ahead. The background music is provided by the bugler, accompanied by the clinking of metal sabres and scabbards with riding tack. From the defenders, there's only silence as they hold their positions under cover to maximise the element of surprise when the time came for their counter defence.

When a cavalry charge is at full gallop, it is nigh impossible to stop the animals racing forward, as was later experienced by General Ponsonby at the Battle of Waterloo. The mounted Corks charged forward towards the ditch with sabres and lances glinting in the mid-day sunlight.

Without warning, the 120 Pikemen of Wexford rose up to meet them, using their pikes and muskets and throwing stones as missiles. The unwitting charging cavalry fell into the trap and were hacked to pieces. Some of the Cork men pleaded to be spared, speaking "*as Gaeilge*", in the mother tongue of Ireland. But no quarter was given by the well-drilled and well-led men from Wexford, who scored a momentous victory.

What a contrast this tragic scene made with the peace and tranquillity of the natural world inhabited by Wordsworth and Coleridge at the time, thought Jack. How can human beings be so calm and appreciative of nature in one place while in another not far away they can act like rabid animals killing each other?

There must be a better way, thought the young Jack Sinnott.

Chapter 3

As an amateur historian, Jack was keenly interested in the turbulent history between his home country and the one where he would eventually make his home.

He worked hard in his final year at St. Peter's College, passing all seven subjects in the public examinations and gaining honours grades in English, History and Geography. He had played the lead role in the school's drama of the year, The Mummy and the Mumps, a farce in three acts by Larry Johnson. On the sporting front, he failed to make the school's Gaelic football or hurling teams but excelled in athletics. On his final year sports' day, he won all the sprint races and triumphed in the long jump and the javelin too.

Jack's mother came from the adjoining county of Tipperary, although in Wexford she might as well have come from India, for the Irish are a tribal people. Jack's father worked as chief clerk in a solicitor's office in the town.

Growing up in their three-bedroom home in Wexford town during the 1940s, Jack and his older brother Alex shared a bedroom, and their younger sister Bridgit had the small room to herself. Alex was two years older than Jack. In truth, Jack was initially a bit of a disappointment when he arrived, since their mother was praying for a girl. But all told, it was a happy household with the emphasis on education and religion. There being no television in those days, the family became eager listeners to English radio programmes on the BBC, with Alex an avid listener to Radio Luxembourg, which mainly broadcast the pop music of the day, and from the late 1930s until the 1960s enjoyed a large listenership in Ireland.

The local cinema provided an escape from the humdrum of daily life, and a key target was to have enough money for the 'flicks' on Sunday afternoon. Sex never reared its ugly head since the girls at the Presentation Nuns Convent School were guarded like Vestal Virgins. Even if a chap got past the nuns, he certainly would not venture to challenge the girls' Irish mothers. But when there's a will there's a way, and although Jack was not a great tennis player he could reach the ball on any part of the court in a flash, so tennis hops were where he discovered girls and thought what a gift they were from God! He never changed his mind on that score.

As is normal, at some point Jack's attention, and that of his parents, turned to careers. Then came a connection that was to have a major effect on Jack's future.

His father's very good friend Tommy Brannigan often casually popped into the Sinnott household for a chat. His mother would offer tea accompanied by her delicious homemade brown bread with homemade strawberry jam. Tommy was a dapper man and quietly spoken. He was below-average height but always kept himself in good shape. In Wexford town he was known as a skilled carpenter, but there was much more to him than that.

Tommy had served in the British Army and had been destined to be assigned to train special operations forces for the assault on the second front in June 1944. But fate intervened when it was discovered he was colour blind, and he was given a medical discharge. He had a wealth of stories from his days as a military man, and Jack was entranced by his tales of unarmed combat and weapons training. As a present for Jack when he was ten years old, Tommy had made an exact scale replica in wood of the American Thompson submachine gun, complete with circular magazine. To Jack, this was the most wonderful toy he had ever received, so precious that he refused to take it outdoors for fear it might be stolen by the older boys.

During his teenage years, Jack went on a few occasions with his father and Tommy to a secluded part of Curracloe beach on the east Wexford coast, a stretch of which was later used for the opening twenty minutes of the acclaimed film *Saving Private Ryan*. There, Tommy set up targets for Jack and proceeded to school him in the art of holding, aiming and firing a 0.22 rifle in the standing and lying positions with controlled breathing.

When Jack was seventeen, Tommy explained how to dismantle his 9mm Browning pistol and how to clean and reassemble it. But as a stickler for discipline, he would not let Jack fire the pistol until he reached the age of eighteen. So, through Tommy, Jack got a uniquely privileged insight into how to safely use black power pistols. In fact, he soaked it up like a dry sponge thrown into the sea, and in his final year at the college, he joined the Cadet Force and was quickly promoted to the rank of Corporal.

Jack's dad, Leonard, known as Len, claimed to be a descendant of the revered Irish rebel and freedom fighter Michael or Mick Sinnott, who fought and died for Irish independence at the Battle of Vinegar Hill in Wexford in 1798. It was meant to be an insurrection against the tyranny of England, with all able-bodied Irishmen, both Catholic and Protestant, called to arms to fight the arch enemy in the form of Lord Cornwallis and his Redcoats. In the event, only "The Boys of Wexford" showed up on the day with neighbouring Kilkenny blacksmiths providing the famous pikes for the pikemen. Lord Cornwallis and his cannon put the poorly armed rebels to flight, and one of their local leaders, Fr John Murphy, led the escape, heading inland and north to Carlow, where he was murdered.

But, fully aware of the practical need for his son to carve out a career and earn his living, Jack's father would say to him 'join the British Army, boy. It'll make a man of you.' Much to his parents' surprise and no little alarm, that is exactly what he did, and after completing his secondary education in St Peter's, he was admitted to the renowned British Military Academy at Sandhurst in Berkshire in England. This turned out to be a wise move, as the two-year training he undertook before being commissioned opened up a whole new world for Jack.

This was a couple of decades before the course was reduced to one year when it was acknowledged that most entrants would already have undergone military training and experience or undertaken a three-year university degree. Back then, Jack's first choice was to serve in the Irish Guards, and his second option was the Queen's Royal Irish Hussars in the days before it was amalgamated into the Queen's Royal Hussars. But generals had different plans for him, and he was commissioned into his third choice, the British Army Intelligence Corps.

After completing his two years at Sandhurst, Jack opted to study the Indonesian language and graduated after seven months, passing the Civil Service Linguist examination, before going on to graduate at the interpreter level.

This was a precursor to his first overseas posting. Based in Singapore, Sub-Lieutenant Jack Sinnott spent much of his time in Borneo on interrogation duties, working closely as an Indonesian linguist with the Malaysian Special Branch Police. "Sub-Lieutenant" was the title he acquired when first commissioned, although some soldiers of that grade are also known as First Lieutenants. The "Sub" stands for Subaltern, and he wears one pip on his shoulder. The next rank up is Second Lieutenant or Full Lieutenant, and he wears two pips.

So Sub-Lieutenant Sinnott became part of a contingent of Commonwealth and British Forces deployed to support the independence of Singapore and Malaysia from threats and attacks from the Indonesian armed forces of President Sukarno who had become president in 1949.

Sukarno had been vehemently opposed to the planned formation of a Malaysian Federation encompassing North Borneo and Sarawak, which were then British colonies. He regarded himself as a liberator of Malaysia and Singapore from British imperialism.

The notion of securing Malaysia's independence appealed to Jack for obvious reasons given his Irish background. He was stationed in the Far East from March 1964 to October 1966. Shortly afterwards, Sukarno was deposed, and a peace agreement signed between Malaysia and Indonesia.

Chapter 4

Justin Chandler, a public-school boy and son of a wealthy farmer from Ardglass at the foothills of the Mountains of Mourne in County Down, graduated from Sandhurst and was commissioned into the Royal Irish Hussars in the same year as Jack. A carefree, good-humoured young man, Justin was a keen horseman who in times gone by would probably have lead cavalry charges but was now confined to fighting from armoured cars. He was what Jack termed "a proper soldier" from a fighting regiment, and they became good friends.

While on operational duties in Borneo, Jack had met up with Justin and some members of his platoon in a bar in the capital, Kuching. Justin was clearly popular with his men, and Jack made a point of talking with each of them and memorising names as best he could, including Sergeant Bill Parker and the company comedian and Scouser, Private Higgins.

Jack had an ulterior motive in so doing, as he wanted to experience what it was like on jungle patrol with the troops. Joining such a patrol would also provide an opportunity for Jack to converse with some of the local villagers who, in the main, were supportive of the British, Australian and New Zealand presence in Malaysian Borneo. So he asked Justin if he could join his platoon and tag along, so to speak, on one patrol. Justin was up for it, but they would need to get approval from the brigade's Commanding Officer, Lieutenant Colonel Murphy.

When the matter was discussed with him, Murphy huffed and puffed, muttering something about "the green slime". This was a widely-used pejorative nickname for the Intelligence Corps. Their role is focused on the collection, collation and interpretation of information that would be of assistance to field commanders in their decision-making in action. Each regiment or corps in the army has a nickname, and the Intelligence Corps were called "the green slime" as they were rarely involved in frontline action.

The Intelligence Corps motto is "Knowledge gives strength to the arm". This is a very accurate summation of their values, as, despite being one of the youngest Corps in the army, in the years after WWII it proved to be invaluable to military planning. With the intense development of computerisation and the growth in importance of cyber security the Corps has been expanded and is now highly-valued by senior military officers at all levels. In sharp contrast, government cuts have meant that several regiments and Corps have been amalgamated.

So, Colonel Murphy's apparent dismissal of "the green slime" was not unusual. But as soon as he was informed that Jack was from Wexford, his attitude took an about-turn. 'Why didn't ye say so first, man?'

As the portly colonel also hailed from Wexford, he decided to celebrate this contact with a fellow Wexfordian by opening a drawer and unleashing three glasses and a bottle of Jameson's finest Irish whiskey. Needless to say, he soon acquiesced to Jack's patrol request.

The following week, Jack was appropriately suited and booted for jungle warfare, armed with a 7.62 mm SLR (self-loading rifle) and his standard-issue officer's 9 mm Browning semi-automatic pistol. He had not been to the jungle warfare school on the Malay Peninsula like most forward infantry troops and their officers had, so this would be a chance for him to watch and learn about jungle warcraft too. Such tours were informative eye-openers for young soldiers and proved to be very useful in controlling the conflict and avoiding another Vietnam. But, despite their usefulness, they were usually uneventful affairs.

The border separating Malaysia and Indonesia in Borneo was the focal point for the conflict in the early '60s that was known as Konfrontasi. Intelligence-gathering and the winning of the hearts and minds of the locals living in longhouses along the border between Malaysian North Borneo and Indonesian South Kalimantan, was a key aspect of the role. Foot patrols moved through the jungles seeking out CCO (Chinese Communist Terrorists) and Indonesian troops who may have infiltrated across the border. The locals were mainly Dayak head-hunters who had not seen a soldier since the end of the Second World War. That said, they always seemed to know when the troops were on the way, no doubt being informed via the good old jungle telegraph which was far more proficient than army issue radios.

Before they set off, Jack was most impressed with Lieutenant Chandler's pitch-perfect briefing to his thirty-man platoon. When Justin asked if there were any questions, after a brief silence, Lance Corporal Rob Cameron, a blunt Scotsman, simply said, 'The boys canna go, sir.'

Justin, a little stunned, in his clipped Sandhurst accent, said, 'What? Why ever not?'

Cameron replied, 'The wee lads ha'ant ad no tae, boss.'

Justin responded immediately. 'Sergeant Parker, organise tea for the men in the canteen. Back at the assembly point in fifteen minutes.'

Jack was impressed by both the professionalism of the company and Justin's decisive, confident leadership. The patrol underway, the men passed through one kampong after another, staying alert at all times.

But after two hours tracking into the jungle and without warning, calamity struck. The crack of rifle fire was heard, and a round came whizzing through the trees to deliver a fatal head wound to Lt. Justin Chandler. Sergeant Parker shouted, 'Take cover.'

Jack froze for a second. His friend Justin was gone. Jack knew this because he had seen dead bodies with similar wounds in the mortuary in Kuching when he was required to identify insurgents killed in action.

Sergeant Parker looked at Jack, and they both knew what had to happen. Jack shouted, 'Bill, you stay with Justin, signal brigade, report our position and enemy contact, request SAS tracker team and medivac chopper for Justin's body.'

Sparks Mullins, the radio operator, was ordered to cover the ambush alley in case the enemy set up a machine gun.

'I'm going forward,' shouted Jack.

Jack's Sandhurst training had kicked in. Attacking an ambush was the established best form of defence. The key was early detection, followed by reflex-type counteraction, a high volume of return fire, and relentless pursuit. This response transferred the pressure onto the enemy. The most effective counter-ambush measures are well- rehearsed immediate action drills and every soldier must know exactly what he is supposed to do.

Instinctively, the men had already flicked the safety catch on their weapons and fired back. They also used smoke grenades to provide cover until they got out of the kill zone. His 7.62 SLR cocked and safety-catch off, Jack charged forward. Amid the chaos, he spotted Private Higgins cowering behind a tree and shouted, 'Get the feck out of there, Higgins, and fight, man.'

Higgins replied, 'Gun jam, boss.'

Jack said, 'Here, take mine, carry yours and follow me.' He then unholstered and cocked his 9mm Browning with confidence, having at Sandhurst won the gold medal for best pistol shot of his year. He continued his dash forward, shouting, 'Left and right firing, move out, men,' He counted the thirteen rounds in his pistol, leaving the customary two in the magazine until he found a safe place to reload.

Again, he shouted out a command. 'Higgins, you fire high into the trees to avoid a blue-on-blue,' code for killing your fellow soldiers by mistake.

The entire platoon had already swung into action, unleashing magazines of 7.62mm rounds into the jungle to the left and right of them while running the gauntlet of the ambush kill zone. This proved too much for the Indonesians, and they began to scatter back over the border.

When Jack reached the point man leading the platoon, Lance Corporal Cameron, he spotted a young Indonesian raising his Kalashnikov assault rifle intending to down Cameron. Without hesitation, Jack fired his remaining two rounds, and the man fell backwards. The Lance Corporal turned and said, 'Thanks, boss, canny shot.'

Jack's training forced him to reload immediately, but his hands shook so violently that he couldn't fit the magazine into the handle of his pistol. Jock Cameron had seen this before with men after their first action and said, 'Let me do that, sir. The lads need you now.'

With the ambush repulsed, the platoon regrouped; the chopper arrived at the designated landing pad, twelve heavily-armed SAS men with tracker dogs alighted, and they were briefed by Jack before they set off on the trail of the escaping enemy and intent on collecting all available evidence. In the melee of battle, retreating troops often leave clues and drop items that can contain helpful information about identities and plans. Dead bodies are searched for intelligence to help build a picture. Injured enemy soldiers are disarmed and patched up to be picked up later.

Job done, Jack and the platoon set off for home.

Chapter 5

Back in Kuching, Sub-Lieutenant Sinnott was not surprised to be summoned to Colonel Murphy's office.

He marched in feeling fairly pleased with his performance given that all but Justin had returned safely. To his surprise, Murphy tore strips off him straight away, saying, 'Now what's this I hear about you charging through the jungle like a demented Lawrence of Arabia? Didn't they teach you anything at Sandhurst? Don't you know that an officer is supposed to control operations and report the contact himself? This is not the Israeli army. Also, you don't use a platoon commander's actual name over the radio. You use his call sign instead, man. Not only that, I've had a bloody delegation from the Hussars in here requesting you be transferred to their regiment and remain as their Platoon Commander. How ridiculous!'

Jack was speechless and could only mutter, 'Sorry, sir.'

Murphy continued, 'OK, now look here, the Hussars' Colonel request that you join them for dinner tomorrow evening, so you will need a number one mess dress. I'm also arranging for you to accompany Justin's body back to his family in the UK. You can have one week's leave back home in Wexford and then get your backside back here pronto.'

Jack simply said, 'Thank you, sir.' He saluted, and did an about-turn to march out.

At the door, Colonel Murphy said, 'One more thing Mr Sinnott, bloody well done, lad,' and winked.

After a long sleep Jack woke the next day and set about writing his report, accounting for every round of ammunition expended by the men. He then turned his attention to finding a mess dress for the dinner in his honour in the evening. To that end, the Quartermaster Sergeant managed to beg, borrow and steal the necessary clothes from other Intelligence Corps officers permanently stationed in Kuching.

The dinner was really a big "thank you" for saving the life of Hussar Lance Corporal Jock Cameron. But Jack was soon to be taken away by other, more pressing, duties.

Halfway through the main course, the Hussars' Lieutenant Colonel Lumsden received a message, stood up and said, 'Gentlemen, I'm afraid we have to bid farewell to our guest of honour tonight, Mr Sinnott. The Indonesian soldier he dispatched in the jungle has survived and is in Kuching hospital. Surgeon Major Stack is offering the opportunity for some light interrogation before he operates on the patient who will most likely die anyway from the wounds in his stomach and knee. Mr Sinnott, we thank you again, and my driver will take you to the hospital now.' As Jack departed, all officers stood up and applauded him.

At the hospital he learnt the name of the soldier was Batubara. He was twenty-one years old and a paratrooper from the famous RPKAD Indonesian Regiment, the equivalent of the American Airborne Division. Surgeon Major Stack was wearing number one mess dress with medals and had been called away from a performance of Shakespeare's Hamlet given by a travelling group of actors from Stratford-upon-Avon.

Stack had obviously been wined and dined before the theatre and was in high spirits. Referring to the prisoner, he said, 'He's unlikely to survive but we will give it our best shot.' After questioning the unfortunate Batubara, Jack reported that he claimed there was no food and that he was hungry. The surgeon major said, 'Ask him where he got the rice I can see in his stomach.' Jack thought him a brave young man.

After some routine questioning, he left the hospital, tired and emotional after all that had transpired, but remembered to say a little prayer for both Justin and paratrooper Batubara.

Jack met with Justin's family when he attended the military funeral in County Down. While there, his promotion to acting full lieutenant came through, and it was also announced that he was being awarded an MID (Mention in Dispatches) for his action in Borneo. After the funeral, Jack travelled to Belfast and took a flight to Dublin, from where he headed home by bus to Wexford.

His hometown now seemed a world away from Borneo and Singapore. It was November; the air was cold and damp. He met up with some of his school pals, most of whom had found jobs in banks.

They were keen to know how he liked Hong Kong, as most people assumed that those who went out east went to Hong Kong. After a while, Jack stopped correcting them and just said, 'It's very interesting.' He soon realised that it was very difficult for those who had never travelled beyond London to relate to cultures and countries abroad. One day in the High Street, he bumped into some of the girls from the tennis club. *It's amazing what four years and bright red lipstick can do for a young lady,* he thought. They were like bees around a honey pot. When Siobhán Burke asked him why he joined the English Army instead of the Irish Army, Jack made some excuse about opportunities to travel. Frances Roberts asked him why he had lost his Irish accent, considered a treacherous crime in Ireland. You can be forgiven in Ireland for the most heinous crime, but

'Thou shalt not lose your Irish accent!' Actually, in the UK everyone knew Jack was Irish as soon as he spoke, and now back home he was pronouncing his words correctly, ditching the 'dis' and the 'dat' for this and that. This too could be considered an offence.

His dad arranged for Tommy Brannigan to drop by to see how his boy had turned out. Whenever his mother was around, Jack played down the events in the jungle and described his duties as an observer well away from the action. When asked why he was awarded the MID, he said it was for his use of the Indonesian language. In confidence, he shared the ambush details with Tommy just before he left.

After the week in Wexford, he flew back to headquarters in Phoenix Park in Singapore and resumed his role in intelligence-gathering through interrogation. The young man he'd shot survived the major operation at Kuching Hospital and was left with a bad stomach wound and a smashed knee. For the next six weeks, Jack met with him at the hospital for debriefings.

Over the following two and a half years, Jack would alternate his time between Singapore and Malaysia, travelling to Borneo, Brunei, Labuan Island and Kuala Lumpur. Whenever he encountered the Hussars, he was feted at their mess, for they believed his action saved many of their men's lives. But he hated being called a hero, arguing that it was what he had been trained to do. On another occasion Jack was tasked with broadcasting a message to a group of Indonesian soldiers who had been routed by the fearless Gurkhas in the Borneo jungle. The Gurkha Regiment was somewhat of an anomaly in the British Army and a hang-over from colonial days.

The Gurkhas come from Napal and consider it a great honour to be selected to serve in the British Army and are renowned for their discipline and courage.

During Jack's time in Singapore, a Gurkha soldier, Lance Corporal Rambahadur Limbu, was awarded the Victoria Cross for storming an enemy position in Borneo and rescuing two comrades under heavy enemy fire. He retired as Captain Rambahadur Limbu VC.

To deliver his message to the Indonesian soldiers, Jack set off in a Malaysian Air Force fixed-wing twin-engine aircraft with large speakers attached under the wings. These had been used to good effect in the Malaysian emergency in the '50s.

Jack had written a short, sharp two-line message with just the bare essentials. This had to be vetted by the legal eagles at HQ in Singapore but it came back as an eight-line paragraph which he then had to broadcast to the insurgents, urging them to lay down their arms and surrender. A number did and were brought in for interrogation, so he had the opportunity to ask them if they had heard his message from the air. They said they had heard parts of it.

The aircraft was travelling at 120 knots, equivalent to 138 miles per hour; do the maths! (Whenever an American used their term 'do the math,' Jack used to tell them, 'You only have one math, we have lots of maths!')

He had other duties elsewhere too. To prevent incursions from Sumatra, the Royal Navy minesweeper HMS Dartington patrolled the Straits of Malacca. So Jack was charged with accompanying them on one occasion in case they picked up suspects crossing from Sumatra to the Malay Peninsula. In the event there were none, but six insurgents were captured crossing into Singapore from Bantu Island while Jack was at sea. This would keep him busy working with the accommodating Special Branch Police in Singapore. He would also soon be occupied on another front, this one a far more personal matter!

Chapter 6

The HQ at Phoenix Park in Singapore collated all the intel gathered, including Jack's reports. The building housed the British Army top brass concerned with assisting Malaysian Armed Forces to deal with the Indonesian Konfrontasi. For security reasons, the wives and daughters of British military and civilian expats held most of the admin support roles. Many of these were stunningly attractive young ladies bronzed by the constant sunshine on the island.

Military life was indeed exciting for a young man in Singapore in the early sixties, but it was also beneficial to step outside every now and then to see how the other half lived. So in order to provide himself with a stimulating focus during his downtime, Jack joined the Singapore Stage Club, having done some amateur dramatics at St. Peter's College back in Wexford.

It was not long before Jack's head was turned. One grey monsoon Monday morning, staff in the office were feeling a little down after the weekend and dressed again in their unfashionable, dull jungle green uniforms. It reminded Jack of an old black-and-white movie scene.

Then just around eleven a.m., in walked this vision of loveliness, as though someone had switched the scene to technicolour. She was dressed in a pink pencil skirt with a waist the circumference of a side plate. Her white blouse was unbuttoned just enough to be modest but also to reel you in. Black high heels, blonde hair and a smile to disarm the toughest of men. Everyone stopped what they were doing and looked up. Delicately, demurely shy Penny Parsons then walked straight over to Jack's desk and asked if he was Lieutenant Sinnott, knowing full well that he was. Somewhat dumbstruck, he nodded as she handed him his mail. He could not help wondering why a GII Intelligence Colonel's secretary was delivering the mail to a junior officer. Her task complete, she turned, smiled and disappeared as smoothly as she had appeared.

Two days later he bumped into Penny again, and this time he asked her if she would like to accompany him to the ballet at the Opera House in downtown Singapore the following Saturday evening. A little embarrassed, and with her head slightly bowed, she said, 'Yes.'

He knew from the Stage Club of all the coming events at the Opera House, and he assumed that his choice event would impress her. He had never been to a ballet himself, and subsequently he found out that neither had she. As it turned out, they both hated the ballet but had a wonderful evening.

Years later, while standing outside the Grand in Plymouth, Penny Sinnott, nee Parsons, noticed how the entrance to the Grand and its steep set of eight steps and the imposing black lacquered front door. The scene instantly recalled for her that magic moment when Lieutenant Jack Sinnott took her hand as they walked up the steps to the Opera House in Singapore.

Chapter 7

After his six years, military service, Captain Jack Sinnott was offered a position in the Diplomatic Corps, now known as the British Foreign Office. This is not an uncommon career route for former Intelligence Corps men and women. Initially he worked in Chancery at Embassies in Asia and Eastern Europe. He also acted as Assistant Military attaché in the FO while studying for various civil service examinations. Because of his background, he usually ended up in a support or Assistant Military Attaché roles.

It was also necessary for Jack to maintain some military connection and training, given the requirement for him to serve as a Reserve Captain for six years after his retirement from the Army. This gave him the valuable opportunity to update his military knowledge of modern weapons. The Browning pistol had now been superseded by the German Glock 19, which he regarded as a work of art, since there is virtually no kick-back when you fire. The reliable 7.62mm SLR rifle was replaced by the not-so-reliable SA80 using the 5.56 x 45 mm rounds and subsequently replaced by the SA80 A2 and A3 versions.

He was also conscious of other responsibilities. Having married Penny while he was stationed at the embassy in Jakarta in Indonesia, their twin daughters, Jennie and Rebecca, were born, and they spent their early years in Jakarta living at the embassy compound.

As part of another assignment in Japan, Jack was asked to meet with a contact in one of the many tunnels in Japan along the Izu peninsula.

This contact was designated low-risk, so he decided not to carry a weapon. Having parked his car in a secluded spot near one end of the tunnel, Jack followed his instructions and walked alone to the centre of the tunnel, where he was to wait to receive a cache of specific documents.

As they are elsewhere, tunnels in Japan are cold, darkish places with very little light and trucks and cars flashing past. After waiting for twenty fruitless minutes, he was about to abandon the mission when he heard some voices from about two hundred yards away at the other end of the tunnel. As soon as someone enters a tunnel, all you can see is a black silhouette against the background circle of light at the far opening, so he could barely make out two figures, one taller than the other. As they drew nearer, their features became a little clearer, with one a short, round-faced, overweight, mature Japanese man and the other a younger, tall, skinny fellow.

On reaching Jack, the pair stood either side of him and made the usual cultural gestures, bowing and conversing in Japanese. Jack could see that the younger one seemed edgy, reminding him of a young colt on his toes before a race. The older one said, *Genki des ka?* (are you well?) with a Japanese smile and a bow that told you nothing. The younger one was growing increasingly uneasy. He fumbled in his jacket, pulled something out of his pocket, and threw it across towards the short tubby one and then turned and ran. But as the object flew across in front of Jack, he instinctively caught it in mid-air and subconsciously registered that it was a Glock 19 with which he released a double tap (two rounds) to the head of the stocky older man, who immediately collapsed to the ground.

Jack immediately raced back to his car and drove non-stop for ten miles. He then made a phone call and listened carefully to his instructions. That afternoon he was on a flight to Hong Kong, transferring to a British Airways flight to London and a new assignment. Penny and the twins followed a week later.

After Japan, Jack worked at the Foreign Office in London, where he met up with some old friends from the Army. Penny felt he had done enough running around the world and that it was time for him to settle down. The twins, Jennie and Rebecca, were coming towards the end of their primary education years and were soon due to move on to secondary school.

But after three years settled in London Jack decided he had enough of foreign diplomacy and wanted to make a change. So, he retired from the FO and joined an American insurance company, working at an office in the Financial City in London. He had little knowledge of insurance, but as a data analyst, his skills were highly prized in the financial world. He specialised in one area of insurance risk, the Private Client Group. This area was dedicated to covering high nett-worth or very wealthy individuals who wanted to ensure their portfolios, which might include properties, yachts, gold bullion, jewellery, artworks, motor vehicles, in fact, anything that had a high monetary value.

The financial sector needed people like Jack with the data analysis and investigation skills to determine the credibility of the clients and verify that the items they sought to insure actually existed and were owned by them. He also became involved in investigating loss claims made by clients.

After two years he became so adept at detecting fraud that the company wanted him to relocate to New York and work from downtown Manhattan on worldwide risks. But Jack declined the offer and instead suggested he could do it from London. The company agreed and promoted him to Executive Vice President of his specialist business sector.

He was generously remunerated for his efforts, although the position involved a substantial amount of worldwide travel, much to Penny's chagrin.

Chapter 8

Commissioned by Mr John Pethick, the Grand Hotel has been described as one of the fabulous buildings of Plymouth, having been designed by Alfred Norman, an architect from Devonport who also designed Plymouth's Guildhall. The Grand was completed in 1879 and still stands proudly and prominently, south-facing, on the western end of Plymouth's Hoe Promenade.

Plymouth Hoe is set high on a limestone outcrop overlooking Plymouth Sound, a vast expanse of water between the Hoe and the breakwater four kilometres to the south. The Sound is caressed by land to the east called Staddon Heights and to the west by Mount Edgecombe estate. Drakes Island, at one time called St. Nichols' Island, is located a stone's throw from the shore on the west side of the channel leading to the dockyard. It all combines to create a scene that can best be compared to a painting that changes frequently with the seasons and the weather. The variety of traffic on the water includes fishing trawlers, leisure craft, children's sail training groups, paddle boarders, daily ferries from Spain and France, and an array of naval ships and submarines and their supporting tugs and tenders heading to and from the famous Naval Dockyard upriver or to anchor inside the breakwater on massive yellow steel buoys.

On Friday evenings the sailing clubs emerge with their multi-coloured spinnakers tacking and dodging to see who can navigate around the race marks and get back to the club house first for a pint or two.

The Hoe is equally well-known for the probably apocryphal story that Sir Francis Drake played his famous game of bowls there in 1588 while waiting for the tide to turn before sailing out with the English fleet to engage with the Spanish Armada.

During the WWII years, Lady Astor MP worked tirelessly to support the people of Plymouth. She even organised music and dancing on the Hoe for people of all ages in defiance of Hitler's Luftwaffe bombers. A modicum of navigation knowledge makes the scene even more interesting. The area is festooned with navigation marks and their flashing lights at night. At the east end of the Hoe, you can look down on Sutton Harbour and the steps from where the Pilgrims are thought to have left to board the Mayflower, a European cargo ship bound for the New World in September, 1620.

The historic locality known as the Barbican has become a bucket list item for tourists visiting Plymouth. It used to house the old fishing quay and the former site of the auction house, which has since moved to the other side of the harbour, which in turn has been modernised to accommodate larger trawlers than it used to. So, there is no shortage of history attached to Plymouth.

Originally a seventy-seven-bedroom hotel, the Grand's guest list over the years is impressive too. It is widely reported that such eminent celebrities as The Beatles, Laurel and Hardy, and ex-Prime Minister William Gladstone all stayed there. What is not so widely known is that a man named Frederick Bailey Deeming, a notorious killer born in Leicestershire, was a guest at the Grand together with his pet cub lion, which he had brought back from Africa. He was later convicted and executed for the murder of a woman in Melbourne, Australia. But he is also remembered today because he was suspected of being the notorious serial killer Jack the Ripper. Nor would he be the last visitor to the Grand to be suspected of a heinous crime.

In the early days of the hotel, the first floor had keyed round arches on polished granite columns. These were set on plinths between turned balustrades and were open to the elements and the prevailing south-west winds. Later, these were fitted with sash windows that are there to this day.

And so, this imposing building remained as one of the prime landmarks of Plymouth until calamity struck, and events at the Grand Hotel found their way into the local and national media, bringing the noble building the kind of publicity most commercial organisations would prefer to avoid.

The trouble started on Sunday, 7 September, 2003, when fire services from Devon and Cornwall were alerted to an incident at the Grand Hotel at about eleven forty-five a.m. A fire had apparently started in the west end of the building on the top floor occupied by the chambermaids and other live-in staff.

The fire raged while onlookers watched aghast from the Hoe, and flames and smoke could be clearly seen from Staddon Heights Golf Club to the east of Plymouth Sound. The firefighters brought it under control by pouring gallons of water into the building to drench the inferno and prevent it spreading. The damage to the building was in major part due to water leaking down through the building.

In the days and weeks that followed, the denizens of Plymouth speculated as to how the fire started. Might it have been caused by an electric fault? Or a lighted cigarette? Some of the speculation was plausible, some not.

Either way, the chambermaids lost their jobs as a result of the damage, and some blamed their battle-axe head housekeeper known as "Nosey Esther". She was a very private person and did not discuss her personal affairs with the staff in her charge. On occasions they would see a young child mysteriously going into her room on the top floor, but she never explained who or why.

In due course, a fire-sale presented an opportunity for a seasoned developer to step in. He persuaded Plymouth Council that he could restore the building as a luxury apartment block while maintaining its original elegance. After many meetings, planning permission was granted, and support from commercial banks was relatively easy to secure. This was to be developer Charles Bartlett's masterpiece, a Grade II listed apartment block on the prestigious Plymouth Hoe. He later added fuel to the fire, as it were, by reinforcing the theory that the inferno was probably caused by a careless housekeeper who smoked like a chimney.

The Grand was subsequently converted into twenty-six superb high-spec two and three-bedroom apartments during the years 2007 to 2010. The impressive conversion did indeed retain the elegance of the original building, not just with the restored exterior but also with a gracious reception hall and common areas furnished in keeping with the original style. Modern lifts and facilities were installed, and the apartments were configured to the demands of contemporary living.

It was very much to the credit of the developer that he had the vision to re-capture the elegance of the Victorian era.

As Jack and Penny were to discover, a characteristic of the residents in the newly-refurbished Grand is that one or both of each couple had some prior connection with Plymouth. In the case of the Sinnotts, it was Penny's hometown. They were seriously attracted to one of the three apartments that had a stunning sea view on the west side of the first floor out over the cherry trees in the front garden. It was a coveted location that Penny had long desired but never imagined she would own.

They moved in two weeks before Christmas Day in December 2010, and were both delighted with their move.

Chapter 9

Even after the Sinnotts settled into their apartment in the Grand at 24 Elliot Street, work was still on-going to complete the remaining apartments so they could be handed over from the builder to the developer. This is a key event in the development of a building, in that the developer or new owner becomes liable for service fees and ground rent at that point. Once handed over, even if the apartment is not sold, the developer must fund those fees.

The builder in this case was an affable man called Paddy Lynch. He was from Donegal in the most northwesterly part of Ireland. Lynch was one of the many Irishmen who came to rebuild Britain after WWII, leaving home at the age of seventeen to seek work labouring on building sites. Untypically, he did not drink alcohol, and unsurprisingly he ended up with his own successful construction company. He set up shop in a space on the lower ground floor of the building at 24 Elliot Street and it became the nerve centre of the operation.

Danny's family were tunnellers by trade and were responsible for building many railway tunnels in England and Scotland. His company, Lynch Construction Limited, was involved in a number of building projects with the developer of the Grand, Charles Bartlett. Much praise had been heaped on Bartlett for the restoration job he achieved with the Grand and with justification. Great attention had been paid to detail. As an example, the design called for a match for the original lincrusta (heavily embossed wallpaper) below the dado rails. So they diligently sourced the company that had the original pattern for this design.

Charles Bartlett exuded all the charm and bonhomie of the polite English gentleman. He and his charming wife Madeline, or Maddie as she liked to be called, lived outside Taunton in Somerset. She was listed as a director of the Grand Management Company and entertained guests visiting the building. For the summer months, they usually retired to their villa in Portugal.

A large, stout man, he was clean-shaven with a thick shock of white hair brushed back and curling up from his collar. It actually reminded Jack of a breaking wave foaming at the water's edge on Curracloe beach back in his native Wexford. Conscious of his appearance at all times, Bartlett always sported a floppy silk handkerchief from his top pocket. He wore the mandatory powder-blue chiffon scarf double-folded to create a ruff-like collar around his neck. A confident man, he had a tendency to dominate conversations, constantly smiling, laughing and making jokes. He was a somewhat larger-than-life theatrical character in many respects. Always charming to the ladies, he gave off a sense of nothing being too much trouble to him, and his answer to nearly all questions was 'Yes.' He would see to it that it is done, so much so that Penny said, 'He would yes you to death.'

Like many seasoned developers, Bartlett was accustomed to dealing with complaints from new residents after they moved in. Developers are heroes when everything works well, but when something goes awry, they become public enemy number one. For the most part, Bartlett was fair and eventually sorted most of the minor issues.

Delivering on promises was not always a simple matter. Bartlett had set up the company Devine Homes Limited to develop the Grand and assigned the marketing of the apartments to a local estate agent. This meant that the financial control of the development was ring-fenced within Devine Homes Limited. The financing of the project is regularly provided by a bank, and whenever new situations arise that require extra funds, the developer must go cap-in-hand to the bank to make a convincing case for the unplanned additional expenditure.

They say that moving to a new home is one of the most stressful things we do in life, but there can also be stresses for the developer that are unseen by the new occupants.

Bartlett had a good reputation for developing properties in Devon and Cornwall, but the Grand was his piece de resistance. As a Grade II listed building, great care had to be taken to retain the ambiance of the Grand of old, not least because it was demanded by Plymouth Council planning authorities. Bartlett was rightly proud of his work, and the local council were pleased with what had been an eyesore on the Hoe since the fire had been transformed into twenty-six luxury apartments of different shapes and sizes. They had been finished to a very high specification with all the elegance and charm of the Victorian hotel era. Not only that, but other buildings in the surrounding streets seemed to get a new lease of life, with some being redeveloped and others cleaned up and redecorated. The Grand was the spark that lifted the whole area around it.

When asked what caused the horrendous fire Bartlett usually replied that it was probably a lighted cigarette by a careless employee. When Jeff Robins, who occupied number thirteen on the second floor, once overheard him say this, he asked Bartlett if there was any real evidence to support that assumption. Bartlett said, 'No, but you know how careless people can be.'

Jeff said, 'Well, I guess their loss is your gain,' at which Bartlett grinned and changed the subject. An apartment block like the Grand usually has a landlord who owns the freehold title to the building through a separate company. Those who purchase apartments become leaseholders for a defined number of years. In the case of the Grand, it was nine-hundred-ninety-nine years. The leaseholders pay an annual ground rent to the landlord as well as an annual service fee to maintain the building. The service fee includes a contribution to a reserve or sinking fund set up to deal with emergencies and longer-term maintenance issues. The administration of all this is usually handled by a management company. The directors of the management company are drawn from the residents who in turn employ a managing agent to deal with the day-to-day administration of the company.

So, a managing agent from nearby Plymstock had been appointed to administer the building. This company was run by a young man who was very knowledgeable about property management. The freeholder or landlord who received the ground rent was a company called Solarhaven Limited. Bartlett said he did not own the company, but his family had an interest in it.

Jack and Penny were pleased to learn that a doctor was moving into apartment number six on a level just below them. Young Philip Hoskin worked at the local hospital at Derriford on the edge of Dartmoor. A charming young man whose passions included fast cars and even faster lady friends, he worked extraordinarily long hours like many in his profession. Initially he had relatively little furniture, but was gradually sorted out by his parents who came and went for a few weeks until he settled in. He did not have a sea view but was not bothered by this since he mainly used the apartment for sleeping.

It's normal for apartment blocks and housing estates to organise regular meetings at which resident members can get to know each other and discuss matters of mutual interest. The Grand was no different, and in due course there would be much to discuss.

The management board initially consisted of two directors, Charles Bartlett and his wife Maddie. He was at great pains to point out that they had what he termed "the Golden Share". This meant that they could not be outvoted by the residents on any matter until all apartments were sold. This is not common practice, but from a developer's viewpoint, it gives him control and protection until a building is completed and all apartments are sold.

After Jack Sinnott had completed the sale, he met Bartlett at a party in the Gladstone Room. Jack introduced himself with his usual direct approach, getting straight to the point by asking him, 'Have I done everything that the contract says I am supposed to do with respect to legal completion and payments?'

Bartlett was a bit taken aback by this and said, 'Well, yes, as far as I am aware.'

Then Jack said, 'Right, so now I expect you to do everything that you are supposed to do. So let's start with the size of the sinking fund for on-going maintenance and refurbishment of this beautiful building.

'From documents I have read, the reserve or sinking fund is set at £5,000 per annum, so over five years we will have amassed £25,000.

'How far do you think that will go in redecorating this building externally and internally in five years' time?'

Taken aback again, Bartlett replied, 'Oh, is that what it is? I wasn't aware.' He then called for one of his assistants and asked him to have a look at the reserve fund for him and then changed the topic of the conversation. Jack had encountered a similar experience in London, where the sinking fund was inadequate, forcing residents to dig deep into their pockets to fund a new roof.

Right away, both Bartlett and Sinnott knew that this was going to be a business-like relationship and not a marriage made in heaven.

Chapter 10

With the bit between his teeth, Jack set about having some residents as directors on the Board of the Management Company and putting in place some ground rules. The managing agent, appointed in advance by Bartlett, recommended that two residents, Bill Penberthy and Jack, be appointed as board directors, making a total of four but retaining the stipulation that the Bartletts could still not be outvoted.

At the first Annual General Meeting, Jeff Robins, who occupied number thirteen, introduced himself to Jack and Penny. Originally, the building was not intended to have a number thirteen, but Jeff insisted that it should. He especially liked living in the Grand and found it a haven from the busy hustle and bustle of Plymouth. His wife, Dr Corinne Robins, was rarely around as she worked on the oil rigs in the North Sea, having graduated from Cambridge with a Doctorate in Petroleum Geology.

Jack proposed raising the reserve fund from £5,000 to £26,000 per annum. Residents took a deep breath, realising that this would mean £1,000 per apartment every year just for the sinking fund. Jack explained that it was essential to build a substantial reserve fund for emergencies and major projects in the future. One resident was quite vocal and said that he agreed with the logic of the proposal and even queried if £26,000 per annum would be sufficient. The meeting voted in favour of Jack's proposal.

But Jack, who had much experience of the workings of the corporate world, was appalled at the running of the meeting and Bartlett's sneering attitude to his suggestion that they approve the re-appointment of the auditor for the coming year which is normal best practice at an AGM. Suggestions from the floor were all welcomed by Bartlett, only for him to then delegate responsibility for implementation to the builder who was an obliging man provided he received funding in advance of any work. This was not at all satisfactory for Jack or the other residents.

The residents were aware that the aftermath of the 2008 financial crash had begun to take its toll on construction and developing in the building industry, and this added a degree of urgency to their concerns. At the time of the meeting, only six of the twenty-six apartments in the Grand had sold. Bartlett agreed that they were 'sticking a bit', which was a serious understatement.

Jack remained quiet for most of the meeting until it came to AOB (any other business) when he asked Bartlett who was going to pay the service fees and reserve fund contribution for the apartments that had been completed and handed over by the builder but which still remained unsold. Jack pointed out that this is usually the responsibility of the developer. That brought an instant frown to Bartlett's face as if this was the first time he had ever been challenged on this point in a new development. But he had no option but to agree, and with a smile, he admitted that he would have to pick up the tab. In reality, it was the bank that would fund it.

After the meeting, Jack approached Jeff Robins and asked if he would be interested in joining the board as a director. Jeff hissed and puffed, saying, 'No, no, no,' as he was already far too busy and had no real interest in committees. He then rushed off.

Jeff was a first-class honours graduate who gained his Doctorate in Quantum Physics from Cambridge where he met his wife. A quiet man aged about forty, he worked for the Ministry of Defence and sometimes lectured at Plymouth University. Thin as a rake with a goatee beard, he rarely joined in conversation with other residents but was always reserved and pleasant. When he did speak, he tended to hiss and blow and puff like an old generator starting up. But he was passionate about the Grand and always interested in any developments being undertaken. He seemed a little eccentric to some, an introvert and a keen jogger who was sometimes seen out at one a.m. running around the Barbican and the Hoe. In conversation he rarely criticised others, although he made a clear exception with the developer Bartlett. In fact, there appeared to be some bad blood between Robins and Bartlett, and he had ominously warned Jack, 'Watch your step with Bartlett.'

Jeff and his wife would regularly buy two copies of The Times and compete to complete the crossword first. Theirs was a childless marriage. When she was in Plymouth, they appeared to have a spiky relationship and on occasions were heard shouting at one another.

Bill Penberthy and his charming wife Louise were Plymothians through and through. Bill had a very successful career in building high-spec luxury yachts and selling them to wealthy international clients. Like most couples in the Grand, they were happily retired and within easy reach of their offspring and their grandchildren. Bill fully understood the complexities of the leasehold relationship with a landlord and the role of the property management company. He also had a sound knowledge of Plymouth and the market for property.

Bill and Louise suggested organising an informal get-together of all the residents so that everyone could meet their neighbours. Jack was always amused whenever he saw the reluctance of the English to socialise unless they had already been introduced. Bill prepared a circular to inform all residents that he planned to hold a BBQ in the garden on a Saturday two weeks hence.

On the day, Bill organised a small gas-fired barbecue in the front garden, while Louise handled the flipping of the burgers. Other ladies prepared finger food and salads, and Penny Sinnott made her celebrated strawberry-and-cream meringue dessert. A selection of bottles of wine purchased at Aldi also adorned the trestle table set up in the garden. Those who liked to sit down brought camp chairs.

Shaded by the famous cherry trees, a number of residents gathered around the table in a semi-circle. The sun shone, but the temperature was cool, to say the least.

A small bald, rotund man called Andy Mole, who lived in number twenty on the 3rd floor in the east wing, did his best to cheer everyone up.

Andy was perfectly affable, good-humoured gentleman, but his wife Alice had sadly passed away some ten-years earlier, and he regularly visited her grave in Efford Cemetery nearby. Andy and Alice used to enjoy coach trips to Europe in the summer and would regale people with their photographic slides of buildings in Prague, Hungary, Poland, Bulgaria and elsewhere around the continent. They loved the atmosphere of the cafés in the East European cities. Andy was also knowledgeable about Plymouth, having worked in the dockyard all his life. He took great interest in the comings and goings in the Grand and always made a point of getting to know new arrivals. Some were appreciative of this, but others thought him a little intrusive.

He used to administer the scheduling of arrivals and departures of warships to and from Plymouth Dockyard. But with the advent of computerisation and finding technology all too complicated, he retired. He was a well-known figure at the nearby Plymouth Hoe Bowling Club and the Conservative Club across the road from the Grand. In a sense, the occupants of the Grand became his adopted family. He was popular and courteous to all who lived in the building and willing to help people in any way he could. Approaching his 76th birthday, he complained of a twinge in his right hip. He said he was born in Saltash, a town in south Cornwall, and his parents were from Cornwall. Jack thought his accent was a strange mixture of Cornish and Devon.

Another resident, Claudia Fernsby (nee Wildbore-Smythe), had recently retired from her role as magistrate in the Plymouth

Magistrate's court. This gave her an air of authority way beyond her current station in life. She had decided that some greenery might add a touch of panache to the barbecue, and she and her husband, George, had turned up with a cactus plant.

Claudia was short in stature and always well-groomed. She always stood out in a crowd thanks to the signature folded wrap she wore over her left shoulder. She had an array of these items in various colours and designs, which she produced whenever she felt the occasion demanded. But this one hardly did. Nevertheless, she marched around wearing a wrap precariously balanced on her left shoulder and wholly inappropriate for a barbecue, with George trailing along behind.

She tended to look people up and down while exuding an authoritative air of "I'm in charge here". On any subject, she would make a link to her own experience and that of her family. Thus, we learnt that her father had been a diplomat and had retired, inheriting the family land in Cornwall. Their land contained two tin mines no longer in use, with the surrounding fields well stocked with sheep. Claudia's brother now ran the sheep farm.

George was a real gentleman now retired from a successful career in marketing double-glazing. Always willing to help those in need, at times he could sound a mite patronising, referring to all men as "old boy" whilst at the same time obeying Claudia's every command. But he meant well.

With glass in hand, Andy Mole called for attention. 'What shall we drink to? Let's drink to the Grand.'

'The Grand,' they all shouted, along with their cheers, nostrovia, and good health.

Sláinte, said Jack, using the usual word for cheers or good health in the Irish language.

Fenekig, shouted Andy.

'Not heard that one before,' quipped Bill Penberthy.

'Oh, it's one I think I picked up in the Czech Republic,' said Andy.

But Jack had covered the Czech Republic in his service years and knew that 'cheers' in Prague is *na zdravi,* a bit like the Russian *naz dorovie,* pronounced in English slang as nostrovia. It means "let's get drunk," so they set about doing exactly that.

Dr Phil popped in before departing for Derriford Hospital. Andy Mole asked if he wouldn't mind having a chat with him about his hip.

'Love to, Andy,' said the young doctor apologetically. 'But must dash. If it's troubling you, why don't you pop down the hill to the surgery, and they'll sort you out?'

'Aye that's what I'll do then. Thanks for the help, Doc,' said Andy.

At that, the doctor waved goodbye to everyone as the ladies swooned, saying what a wonderful young man he was. A few minutes later they heard the roar of his red MG powering down Atheneum Street on its way to the Derriford Hospital.

As things were beginning to wind down, in walked Jeff Robins and his wife, Corinne. They apologised for being late, Jeff explaining that he had to go to Bristol Airport to collect Corinne from her flight from Glasgow. Tall and attractive with long blond hair, Corinne Robins wore a blue trouser suit and practical sports shoes. Jeff introduced her to everyone.

When Corinne towered over Claudia Fernsby, it was obvious that the former magistrate had met her match.

'I believe you work in Glasgow,' said Fernsby.

'No, I don't. Actually, I work on platforms in the North Sea,' Doctor Robins corrected.

Suitably chastised, Mrs Fernsby said, 'How interesting, we have tin mines in Cornwall, and we're hoping one day we might strike oil, *ha ha.*' Corinne merely smiled and walked on.

For some residents, the barbeque had been the first time they had met. Inevitably, much of the chatter was about getting used to the building and how the underfloor heating is programmed and the fact that recent residents were not informed by the estate agent that there were some problems with the render on the south-facing elevation of the building.

Indeed, as each new resident occupied their apartment, there were fresh complaints about damp. Bartlett took the matter seriously and consulted with the architect and the builder who both said that residents needed to be patient and let the building settle and that the render was fine. Andy Mole offered to set the programme for the heating controls for anyone who found them difficult to manage.

So all-in-all, it had been a pleasant and worthwhile gathering.

Chapter 11

Despite the passage of time, a number of the apartments were still in the process of completion. Irritating building noises were compensated for by the fact that the presence of skilled workmen on site meant that small defects could be fixed promptly. The foreman was an obliging man and did his best to accommodate the new arrivals.

Both Jack and Bill were becoming increasingly concerned about damp from the sea-facing side, and they agreed to ask for a meeting with the developer Bartlett. It was proposed that a professional survey should be carried out to assess the extent of the problem. Again, Bartlett agreed that it was a good idea, but given that the residents had requested it, he felt they should pay for it. This did not go down well with Bill and Jack, who were also concerned that apartments were being sold without full disclosure of the serious and justified concerns about the leaking render. After the survey had been carried out, it was confirmed that cracks existed in the render, which in turn allowed water ingress and the resulting damp. Jack and Bill insisted that new purchasers must be informed about the defect and a plan undertaken to rectify the problem.

With the passing weeks, sales slowed further apart from two new arrivals. Lt Col Anthony de Billier Fortescue, a retired Royal Marine officer, and his wife Charlotte moved into the east wing from where he could almost see his old office in the Citadel at the end of the Hoe promenade. De Billier was a military man through and through. He did not suffer fools, nor did he tolerate inefficiency, so it was not long before he clashed with the builder and with Bartlett. Having decided that having a professional snagging check was a waste of money, he opted to do his own snagging list. The problem with that is that sometimes it is not until you live in an apartment for a while that you discover certain types of defects.

Meanwhile, Lynch was still finishing the fit-out of the building and did what he could to help, but some projects were too expensive to correct, so hostilities opened up with Bartlett.

De Billier had seen action in the Middle East, Germany, the Falklands, Northern Ireland and Afghanistan. He had enjoyed a successful career in the military, tinged only with his disappointment at not making it to full colonel status. Not surprisingly, he and Jack Sinnott gelled well together, sharing war stories and occasionally arguing about Northern Ireland over a bottle or two of wine. Jack blamed the Parachute Regiment for facilitating the largest recruitment of young men into the IRA as a result of their actions on Bloody Sunday in Derry in 1972. He had been so incensed that he wrote to the Sunday Times about it, and his letter was published.

Charlotte, de Billier's wife, was a charming lady who regularly exercised their black labrador Jessie on the Hoe. An attractive woman, she was always nicely groomed and had a positive, fun-like attitude to life. She was member of u3a, a UK-wide network of over a thousand charities that provide opportunities for those no longer in work to come together and "learn for fun". Charlotte's special interest was exploring the connection between stories and music. She was an avid reader and an accomplished pianist too, and her subgroup met monthly in a room at the university in Plymouth. The de Billiers had three daughters with different personalities who by now were getting on with their lives in various parts of the country.

Penny and Charlotte became good companions who shared confidences. Both had travelled the world in support of their husband's chosen careers.

In contrast to the high-flying backgrounds of some residents, the colourful Fred Potts, known locally as "Potty", ran a successful second-hand car dealership called "Potty Cars" on the outskirts of Plymouth.

He had served in the Royal Navy for just over eight years until he ran afoul of the strict military discipline. Sadly, he left before completing his nine-year contract, which meant he could not receive a pension.

He was a capable engineer who knew a little about a lot. He was quite open about the buying and selling of cars and acutely aware that he had run close to incarceration in HMP Dartmoor on more than one occasion.

Fred admitted that under no circumstances would he allow his only son Rodney to go into the business, so Rodney was dispatched to Exeter University to study marine biology instead. This was Fred's proudest boast, and he would delight in telling everyone that 'the boy's comin' 'ome soon'. His long-suffering wife Beryl was a down-to-earth, supportive companion to a good-humoured rogue, and a night at the bingo and the odd glass of sherry were sufficient to keep her happy.

It was hard to dislike Fred because of his openness about himself and his deeds and misdeeds. He claimed that he never sold a duff banger to anyone. 'I've 'ad some come back, mind,' he would admit. 'Honest facts, you wouldn't believe what these young people get up to, no respect for a decent motor.'

He was known to the constabulary who often visited him about a car he had sold that might have been involved in some crime or other. On one occasion he was stopped while driving by a young constable who asked him to pull over and then instructed him to blow into a bag.

Fred refused, and an argument ensued. Embarrassed, the police officer said, 'Look, I've broken the seal; now you have to blow into it, Fred.'

Fred said, 'That's your problem, son. I've only 'ad one glass of ale, and you have no reason to stop me.'

'But I can't go back to the station with a broken seal and no reading,' explained the officer.

'Well, you shouldn't have broken it then, should ya?' said Fred before driving off.

He heard no more about the matter.

Over a period of time, Fred had amassed a stash of cash that enabled him to purchase one of the smaller apartments in the Grand. After much to-ing and fro-ing, he realised that you could not just show up with a Trago Mills plastic bag full of £50 notes to pay for it. So, his solicitor helped him to understand the inner workings of property conveyancing.

Like Penny's father Bill, Fred was really a Barbican boy, and given that connection, he could not do enough for Penny. But it was not like that with everybody. On the surface Bartlett and Fred were like chalk and cheese, and the theatrical Bartlett humoured and tolerated Fred and his open book of life-tales. Behind the façade, they were both wily traders with shades of Del Boy and Boycie in the hilarious television comedy series Only Fools and Horses.

Chapter 12

The global financial crisis had hit in September 2008 and coincided with Jack Sinnott's retirement. The build-up to the crisis had lasted for more than five years, but it still took the world by surprise, especially the financial industry, which was at the eye of the storm.

The primary cause of the crisis was the failure of what are termed "risk and derivative financial models". These mathematical models are referred to as algorithms. During one conversation Bill Penberthy asked Jeff Robins to explain exactly what algorithms are.

Jeff did his usual routine of hissing and coughing, but then rolled his eyes to heaven saying, 'Nothing new really. Been around for centuries. Algorithms are merely specific descriptions of step-by-step actions that need to happen to achieve a particular outcome.'

'Ok, I get that,' said Bill, 'but how come everyone is talking about them now?'

'Computers, computers, computers,' said Jeff. 'The advent of computers and their wide availability has made it possible to speed up complex calculations. I assume you are asking because of the financial crisis. The problem is that the assumptions were never properly tested, so policymakers and market participants were inclined to believe that certain investment risks were more secure and more stable than they turned out to be.'

Young upstarts in the financial industry made presentations in boardrooms in New York and London while proffering their algorithms as the new Holy Grail of investing without risk. Blinded by the science, many company directors nodded sagely without truly understanding what they were talking about. Simply put, banks and financial institutions lent money to all and sundry and then packaged the loans in bundles, claiming that they were all triple-A rated.

The risks involved were mainly mortgage loans. The crisis had underlying secondary causes, mainly due to financial institutions that blindly exploited what they believed was a golden opportunity to profit with minimal or no risk. Basically, those who borrowed money could not meet their repayments. These deals had been underwritten or financially guaranteed by insurance companies who were convinced they could not lose money on their investments. Jack had worked for one such company and was relieved that his retirement took him out of the chaos that followed for many such financial institutions.

Whilst the epicentre of the crisis was the United States of America, its negative impact was worldwide. In the UK it impacted property sales, resulting in developers going under as projects failed to meet the lending bank's requirements in terms of financial returns.

The Grand project was not immune from any of this. With only eight of the twenty-six apartments now sold, the bank could no longer fund the project. The get-out for a developer in these situations is to declare his company insolvent. Each major development has its own commercial company, and this in turn protects the developer's personal assets from any involvement in the liquidation of the property. The financial crisis resulted in a downturn in house purchasing and investing as many wanted to "wait and see".

There was an additional major challenge for Bartlett regarding those residents at the Grand with apartments now suffering from water ingress. As the residents blamed this on poor workmanship, Bartlett was seen as being ultimately responsible, so they demanded he fix it.

Sales of apartments almost ground to a halt, a scenario that was devastating for Bartlett. Many developers were in the same predicament, but there was nothing they could do in the short term.

Understandably, the lending bank wanted to see a return for their investment.

Jack Sinnott argued that the insurance company's ten-year guarantee policy should pay for any repairs. But Bartlett scoffed at this idea and said that it was highly unlikely they would agree to pay. As an experienced developer, he was also aware of the subrogation clause in insurance. When there is a validated claim from a client, the insurance company may seek settlement from the builder or the developer in the first instance. They will also claim the developer's bond lodged with the council in the event that the building has not been completed as per finished drawings. Bartlett claimed that he never failed to recover his bond, a real mark of a competent developer.

Residents then suggested that the landlord should pay. This was naive on their part, since maintenance of the building is the responsibility of the residents. But there was also much discussion around why Bartlett himself should fund the repairs. This too was naïve, as he was not personally responsible for the building since it was owned by the development company Devine Homes Limited. For Jack, and Bill this was becoming a serious headache, given that they were directors of the management company and residents looked to them for advice.

After further weeks had passed, events overtook the situation. With the bank no longer willing to support the funding of the project, there remained only one option. At a meeting in Plymouth, attended by Bartlett, the managing agent, the lending bank and an appointed receiver, a decision was taken to place the Grand building into administration.

Stuart Fraser, a small Scottish man with a public-school accent, was the appointed receiver charged with disposing of the empty apartments in the Grand at the best price he could achieve in an already depressed market. When all the apartments were sold, he would then proceed to sell the freehold title of the building previously owned by the landlord, Solarhaven Homes Limited. This was a huge blow for Bartlett, and, despite the issues over the render, most residents felt sympathy for the man who had produced one of the most sought-after apartment blocks in the West Country, if not in the entire UK.

In practical terms, the Appointed Receiver takes total control of the building and uses the proceeds of the sale to reimburse the lending bank and to fund his own expenses. In theory, this implied that Bartlett had no further connection with the Grand. But Fraser used Bartlett to sign legal documents since his name and that of his wife were still listed as directors of the management company.

In return, Bartlett was allowed to use one of the apartments in the East Wing of the Grand as his Plymouth office base. This rankled a little with some residents. Their annoyance was not that the project had gone into receivership, since this was the fate of many companies in the UK at the time, but they were perturbed that Bartlett had yet to deal with the many outstanding complaints, especially the leaking render on the south-facing elevation of the building that was causing extensive damp in many apartments.

Given that they were directors of the management company, Jack and Bill Penberthy were disappointed that they had not been informed about the meeting at which it had been decided to put the Grand into receivership. It was then decided to invite the Receiver to a meeting in the hope that they could form a good working relationship directly with him. Jack and Bill went to great lengths to update him on the problems with the render, pointing out that his chances of selling the remaining eighteen apartments were nil if he did not address the render problems since this potential defect now had to be declared to all interested purchasers. At that meeting, Fraser dismissed the possibility of the insurance company funding the repairs and agreed to set up his own survey of the building and formulate a plan to address the outstanding issues.

Jack's twenty-years in international insurance had given him a sharp understanding of the fine print of contracts, and he knew how to talk with insurance companies in their language. He pointed this out to Fraser, saying, 'I have an insurance contract arranged by Devine Homes Limited that guarantees the repairing of unknown defects in the structure of the building for ten years. I see no reason why they would not pay up since it would be a breach of contract. They'll pay all right. I'll make damn sure they do.'

At which Fraser simply smiled and said, 'Good luck with that.' One crucial problem was that some residents' insurance certificates had not been registered with the company and therefore did not qualify for the payment, which if approved, would be paid to each apartment. Andy Mole was irate at this too and blamed Bartlett, who in turn blamed someone else. So Mole and Fred Potts had to contribute a further £12,000 each from their savings for their contribution to the repairs. Mole complained bitterly to Bartlett, and it was reported that they were heard shouting at one another in the underground car park. Potts threatened the developer with the full force of the law over the matter.

The survey was completed, and a claims adjuster from the insurance company made a report that effectively said that there were defects in the render which were covered by the policy for most residents.

The cost of the repairs reached just under £300,000. The normally gregarious Claudia Fernsby remained uncharacteristically tight-lipped at the next meeting while making copious notes as she observed the reactions of all present. Two days after the meeting, she wrote to all directors and the managing agent applying to become a director, pointing out that her specialist skills as a magistrate equipped her perfectly to be a director or even chairman. The directors considered her application but turned it down on the basis that four directors were adequate at this stage.

However, the real reason for their taking that stance was that Jack and Bill Penberthy believed that Claudia would cause more problems since she was constantly complaining about her own apartment.

Jeff Robins attended all the meetings in the Grand and usually remained quiet, only speaking on rare occasions, often to quietly thank the directors for their work. Otherwise, he would sit at the back of the room completing the Times crossword, ostensibly detached from the chatter and business going on around him.

On one occasion, when the discussion turned to the potential purchase of the freehold, one resident cautioned of the domino effect of people losing interest above a certain level of investment. But a voice at the back said, 'No, the correlation between the co-efficient of x number of people investing at y has shown in research to influence the cohort group positively rather than negatively, moving the core to solidify their participation. Therefore, it is not correct to state that the domino effect will reduce the support for the acquisition of the freehold.'

This rather convoluted explanation brought a deadly hush to the room until Jack spoke, saying, 'Thank you, Jeff, can't argue with that then.' At the end of the debate, the Freehold Purchase motion was passed.

Robins continued to be regarded as an enigma by the residents. On Friday evenings some might see him leaving the building on foot, dressed in a suit and tie at a time when most men were relaxing in casual clothes. One evening Penny Sinnott met him and said, 'You're looking very dapper, Jeff. Off somewhere nice?' He told her he was going to a restaurant for dinner. Wherever he was off to, this seemed a regular event for him, either alone or with Corinne when she was in Plymouth. There was definitely something odd about it that nobody could put their finger on. Meanwhile, much to the chagrin of many residents, Bartlett swanned in and out of the building, exuding his usual confidence. He even parked his Rolls Royce in the underground car park free of charge. To rub salt into the collective wound, Bartlett was still using an apartment as his personal office. The Receiver would continue to use him for necessary signatures on legal papers.

But some took a little consolation that the financial crisis had hit many construction projects hard and that what was happening at the Grand merely reflected events occurring all over the country.

Chapter 13

After Bartlett's body was discovered by Mrs Ivy and Molly, Bill Penberthy explained to the police why Bartlett used apartment number nineteen as his Plymouth office. He also confirmed that the dead man's car was in the car park and set about informing all residents of the tragic development. It was not long before the body was taken away for a coroner's examination.

Although Jack Sinnott and Penny had been in the building at the time, they were unaware of the commotion in the east wing until contacted by Bill. The general opinion was that Bartlett had probably died due to a combination of obesity, alcohol and stress from recent events caused by the global recession. It was common knowledge that many developers and business owners were suffering through equally serious traumatic situations.

That evening Bill suggested he gather everyone in the Gladstone Room to bring residents up to date on events and allow people to absorb the news. He would also reassure them that there was no evidence of foul play or a break-in, and no suicide note, so the most likely scenario was that Bartlett had died from natural causes. All eight of the currently occupied apartments were represented in the Gladstone Room for the meeting.

Claudia Fernsby, complete with her trademark wrap, took great pains to explain the legal procedure in these matters based on her experience as a magistrate. Ever the gentleman, young Dr Hoskin politely corrected her on a few salient points. Jeff Robins asked if Bartlett's wife had been informed, adding that this turn of events would be extremely distressful for her. Andy Mole said that Bartlett had mentioned to him that his wife was at their villa in Portugal and that Bartlett had only returned from there for a week to clear up some matters for the Receiver.

Gloom and shock were the dominant emotions permeating the room. People consoled themselves with the fact that Bartlett was not a resident and no longer had any ownership of the building. There was an unspoken undertone of sympathy, mixed with a tinge of 'well, he could have done more to solve some of the early problems for us' in the attitudes of the residents.

Jack Sinnott listened with interest, his background guiding him to keep an open mind. Life is never quite what it seems at first glance, as he would frequently say to Penny. She and Charlotte sat together in the meeting and made teas, and coffee for all in the room.

Beryl Potts could not stop sobbing openly at the tragic nature of the whole episode. 'He was a lovely man,' she said, 'and always very nice to me. I feel terrible for his poor wife.' Fred put his arm around her and gave her a hug.

The police traced Bartlett's wife, Madeline, through a contact number given to them by the managing agent's office in Plymstock. She immediately made arrangements for returning to the UK, arriving at Bristol airport to be met by her daughter, who then drove her to the family home near Taunton in Somerset. Her son joined them there later in the evening.

The local police, having been briefed by their counterparts in Plymouth, visited her to offer their condolences and update her on progress with their enquiries. She said she had been in Plymouth with her husband only four weeks earlier and that Charles was perfectly fine then. In fact, the appointment of a receiver, whilst a considerable disappointment, was somewhat of a relief as it freed Bartlett to concentrate on his other projects.

Together with her son and daughter, Madeline travelled to Plymouth to identify Bartlett's body and meet with the police there. The body itself could not be released, nor could a funeral be arranged, until the results of the autopsy and the exact cause of death were known.

Madeline Bartlett had been married to Charles for thirty-eight years, and all indications were that it was a trouble-free, happy union. Madeline seemed to enjoy her status in life as the wife of a wealthy property developer. A tall woman about five years younger than Bartlett, she was always impressively groomed and wore expensive clothes. She enjoyed meeting with architects as well as with councillors and other dignitaries, including the mayor of Plymouth. She did not interact so much with the apartment residents, perhaps because she found most leaseholders tended to trouble her with complaints and were not always appreciative of the achievements of her husband.

While in Plymouth, she was invited to meet with Chief Inspector Carson Penhaligon at the nearby police station. He tried to be sensitive to the situation and to show appropriate sympathy for her tragic loss. He enquired about Bartlett's recent health, and she confirmed that the loss of the Grand had been very hard for him, but otherwise he was in very good health. She declared that her husband had arranged a joint will with all assets in the estate passing to the surviving spouse. Consequently, she would be the main beneficiary after the probate process was finalised. Penhaligon asked if she wouldn't mind helping Detective Sergeant Don Akesh to complete a report on her movements since she last visited the Grand. She in turn confirmed that she could be contacted at her Taunton home if needed.

The police requested all residents to give details of their whereabouts during the week leading up to the time the cleaning ladies discovered the body. Residents who worked during the day were interviewed in the evening. Doctor Philip Hoskin in number six only learnt of the incident on return from his shift at Derriford Hospital around seven p.m.

Jeff Robins only heard the news on his return from the dockyard and was visibly shocked to the point of being speechless. Andy Mole shuffled about, shaking his head, saying, 'Poor old Bartlett, he was a decent sort really.'

Chapter 14

Word still had not reached the Herald, Plymouth's local daily newspaper. But Chief Inspector Penhaligon knew it would not be long before the word got out.

He had been with the Devon and Cornwall Police Force since leaving Plymouth Grammar School. A very capable and thorough policeman, he had made his name solving several criminal cases in Plymouth and Devon generally.

He was known in the force as 'Penhaligon of the Dockyard,' since many of the cases over the years had some connection with the Royal Navy or the Dockyard in the Devonport area on the west side of the city. Working in military establishments, Penhaligon matched the smartly dressed naval officers in their uniforms. He usually wore a white shirt and a pinstriped dark suit and a silver-striped dark tie.

The regular shine on his black shoes was well up to the standard of any military parade and had been inspired by his son, who had served in the Devon and Dorsetshire Regiment, where like most of the army, shoe-shining is an art that once learnt only needs simple maintenance.

Penhaligon's grey hair was neatly cut, and he sported a meticulously-trimmed moustache. At 6'3" inches tall, he was an imposing presence when he entered a room. He had a calm temperament and spoke clearly and softly, listening carefully to people's responses while also observing their facial expressions and hand gestures. At sixty-three years of age, his retirement was due within two months, something he looked forward to. Basically, he had served his time, seen it all and wanted a rest so he could spend time with his family.

His recent annual medical check also indicated that it was time he slowed down or his aortic stenosis might catch him off guard. His young assistant, Detective Sergeant Akesh's grandparents came from Islamabad in Pakistan, and his father was a renowned geriatric consultant in King's College Hospital in London. Akesh himself had served as a reserve constable and had continued in that role while reading for his BSc Hons in Psychology with Criminology at Bristol University. For his gap year, he travelled to New York to observe how the police there dealt with crime and carried out their investigations, and he was to apply many of their techniques to solving cases back home. After his studies at Bristol, he graduated at Henley Police College as a fully-trained police constable attached to the Hampshire Constabulary in Portsmouth. He was now considered one of the brightest young men in the force, having proved himself on several criminal cases in the area.

The Bartlett case was his first time to work with Penhaligon, and both policemen were understandably at pains to discover the outcome of the autopsy on Bartlett's body. It was suspected that he died due to asphyxiation and had been dead for about two or three days. That would place the time of death at some time on Friday afternoon when he would normally have been in apartment nineteen anyway. But it was still unclear as to what caused the asphyxiation. With no evidence of a break-in, it was also noted that the door had been locked from the inside. While it seemed very much like a possible suicide, there was no suicide note, no weapon and no evidence of medicines that might have been taken in an overdose. Foul play was not suspected.

Meanwhile, the County Pathologist was awaiting the results of laboratory tests on the dead man's bloods from Severn Pathology, Southmead Hospital at Westbury-on-Trym. He would usually expect to receive the results within a few days, but there appeared to be a delay this time. When DS Akesh contacted the hospital, he was informed that they had sent the details to London Clinical Laboratory to have their findings confirmed.

On the afternoon of the following day, the two detectives arrived at 24 Elliot Street to view apartment nineteen. They made quite a contrast.

Penhaligon was tall and lean with a disarming smile, while the much younger Akesh, after his recent promotion to detective sergeant, was hot on the trail, serious and pushy. They had contrasting personalities too, the former calm and serene and the other as eager as a bloodhound and flushed with confidence following his recent successes.

Residents were again questioned, but this time in much greater depth. Some were a little surprised to see Corinne with Jeff Robins.

She said she had been working in London all week and thought she could come down to see if there was anything she could do to help.

Residents were pleased to see her and welcomed her support at this difficult time. She was due to return to London the following day.

Lynch the builder was located and questioned, not least because he had access to the Grand for the odd jobs he carried out for the Receiver and may even have had a master key. He was also owed some money by the developer for fixing various problems in the apartments.

Most of the residents had some issues with Bartlett, as is often the case with developers, but it seemed highly unlikely they would lead to murder, if that's what it proved to be. There was a string of issues they felt should have been sorted by Bartlett, including his refusal to engage sufficiently with the damp problems on the sea-facing front elevation. The exclusion of Jack and Bill from the meeting at which the appointment of the Receiver was announced and his failure to register some apartments for insurance cover gave residents further grounds for resentment.

When questioned, Lynch the builder, who was a known close associate of Bartlett's and had worked with him on several properties, admitted that he had a key to the building. But in order to carry out work in any one apartment, he would first have had to get the relevant key from the owner or the managing agent. This information was followed up by the police and they were satisfied that no recent request for an apartment key had come from Lynch, and he had not requested the key to number nineteen in the past three months.

Indeed, it was already a couple of months since he had visited the building to carry out some repairs as requested by Fraser.

DS Akesh introduced himself to Jack. 'I understand, Mr Sinnott, that you have an apartment in the west side of the building.'

Jack said, 'Yes, I do. What of it?'

Akesh said, 'I'm just wondering why you were wandering around the east side of the Grand last Thursday.'

Jack was stopped in his tracks and a little stunned by the insinuation that he might have been up to something and tartly replied, 'I live here, so I can wander around any part of the building I like.'

Undeterred, Akesh continued, 'It has been reported that you were specifically seen on the third floor.'

Jack thought quickly and explained, 'As a director of the management company, I was checking to see if there were any signs of damp there.'

'Do you often wander around the east side, Mr Sinnott?' asked Akesh, looking straight into Jack's eyes without saying anything for what seemed like an age.

But Jack recognised this as an old interrogation technique and did not flinch. Then he said, 'I just like to keep an eye on things.'

'Thank you, Mr Sinnott. I may have some more questions for you as part of my further enquiries,' said Akesh before moving his questioning elsewhere, if only for the time being.

Chapter 15

Finally, a full two weeks after the discovery of the body, the results of the pathology analysis came directly to Penhaligon marked "Private and Confidential". It was confirmed that Bartlett had indeed died due to asphyxiation, most likely as a result of a deadly poison in his wine.

Intriguingly, the wine in the glass and in the unopened bottles was contaminated with the same poison.

Penhaligon shared the information with DS Akesh, and they decided that it would be appropriate to communicate these key findings to residents of the Grand. So, he arranged for a meeting in the Gladstone Room for seven-thirty p.m. on the following evening. This would avoid any misunderstanding or the risk of incorrect information leaking out to the media. He also felt that it would be interesting to gauge people's reactions to this news. Prior to the meeting, he called Madeline Bartlett to inform her of the findings of the autopsy report.

She was shocked and horrified and broke down in tears.

At the appointed hour, residents shuffled into the Gladstone Room expecting to find that the case had been solved and that Bartlett had died from natural causes. Claudia Fernsby showed up with a tartan wrap dangling from her shoulder and muttering something to the effect that it was about time we heard the results.

Carson Penhaligon thanked everyone for coming and delivered the stark news that Mr Bartlett had died of asphyxia, most likely as a result of poison in the wine he drank. Gasps of horror filled the Gladstone Room. Beryl Potts, rollers still in hair, began sobbing again.

Most of the ladies in the room had a hand covering their mouths while their eyes were wide open in shock.

To the more astute residents, it was now undeniably clear that Bartlett had been murdered and that the murderer may indeed be living in the building or might even be present in the Gladstone Room at that very moment. It was a breathtaking thought.

Having arranged it in advance, Penhaligon said he would like to ask Dr Hoskin to say a few words about the poison used. Hoskin explained to the still awestruck gathering that aconitine comes from the plant monkshood, which is also known as wolfsbane. Aconitine leaves only one post-mortem sign, that of asphyxia, as it causes arrhythmic heart function, which in turn leads to suffocation.

Poisoning can occur even after touching the plant's leaves while not wearing gloves, as it is very rapidly and easily absorbed into the body.

'The plant has a very alluring purple flower. If you wanted to get away with a murder,' Hoskin explained, 'this poison would be a popular choice due to its untraceable nature. It is said that it has a particularly famous casualty. The Roman emperor Claudius is believed to have been poisoned by his young wife, Agrippina, using aconite in a plate of mushrooms. The poison itself has been known for hundreds of years, but it was not until the second half of the 20th century that clinical pharmacology scientists developed the methodology for identifying aconitine in body fluids.'

At this point Colonel de Billier Fortescue raised his hand and, looking to Penhaligon, said, 'If I may, Inspector, I can verify what Dr Hoskin so expertly explained, as there is also a famous case of the use of this poison in India. During the Indian Rebellion of 1857, a British detachment was the target of attempted poisoning with aconitine by Indian regimental cooks. The plot was thwarted by an Anglo-Irishman, Brigadier John Nicholson, who having detected the plot, interrupted the British officers just as they were about to consume the poisoned meal. The chefs refused to taste their own preparation, whereupon it was force-fed to a monkey who expired on the spot. The cooks were hanged, as you might expect.'

But there was more information to come to tickle the curiosity of the residents. In addition to identifying the poison, the techies in the lab worked out how each bottle of Bartlett's favourite red Sancerre contained the poison even though the bottles still had their corks inserted in their neck, and their foil wrappers intact.

Mrs Fernsby saw another chance to bring matters under her control and asked how on earth could unopened bottles be tampered with and contaminated since even if someone inserted the poison into the bottle, they would need to puncture the foil wrapper, and this would be obvious to investigating police officers.

At that point Colonel de Billier Fortescue turned to Penhaligon yet again and said, 'If I may, Chief Inspector. I do know a little about wine and I think I can explain how the poison can be in the wine without the foil cap being removed.' Penhaligon encouraged him to go ahead, knowing that this offered him another opportunity to quietly observe reactions around the room.

The Colonel explained that it was quite easy to insert a needle into the top of the foil wrapper on a corked bottle without it being detected since there are usually one or two small holes already in the foil wrapper put there to allow the cork to air. As he pointed out, if you examine a decent bottle of wine using a magnifying glass, you can verify this. Wrappers or capsules, to give them their correct title, were originally introduced to prevent rats and mice and cork weevils from enjoying the wine before the master of the house could do so.

'Rats and mice are no longer a threat,' the Colonel added with a chuckle, 'but the capsules are still in use because they probably appeal to the marketing gurus in the wine industry.' He had recently received wine from his supplier in France, where they have dispensed with the wrappers altogether since they serve no useful purpose but merely add to the cost. 'In fact, the use of capsules has become somewhat de rigueur merely in order to separate the supposedly superior wines from the also rans,' he claimed.

'Thank you, Colonel,' said Penhaligon, in turn confirming the practice of inserting air holes in wine bottle capsules and adding that the most likely explanation was that a syringe with a fine needle was used to inject the aconitine solution into the wine directly via the cork.

'Consequently,' he said with some authority, 'we are now investigating a suspected murder, since it is highly unlikely that anyone contemplating suicide would go to the trouble of inserting poison in all three bottles of wine.'

The chief inspector stressed that the police were now focusing on the issue of motive and asked people to consider if they knew of anyone who may have had a motive strong enough to carry out this murder.

'I am aware that there were a number of complaints about Mr Bartlett and that the building had been put into administration, but whilst this may be a factor, it equally may have nothing to do with the murder at all,' he concluded.

The air of quiet gloom that had settled on the assembled small community was broken when someone in the corner spoke up and said, 'Yes, I know who had a strong motive. Me.' It was Fred Potts, and he admitted that he had the motivation to kill Bartlett and that he had told his wife Beryl a few times that he would like to strangle Bartlett over the insurance mess-up.

'Honest facts,' Potts said. 'I was furious about the insurance, see. I'd a killed the bugger with me bare 'ands like, but poison and needles and all that stuff is not me style.'

The truth was that just about everyone here had a reason to be unhappy with Bartlett. But would it be enough to engage in murder?

Probably not, thought Bill Penberthy.

A couple of days later, the Plymouth Herald had the scoop and ran the bold headline on the front page, MURDER AT THE GRAND DEVELOPER DIED FROM LETHAL POISON.

The article went on to say that well-known Chief Inspector Carson Penhaligon confirmed what newspaper sources had reported, that the police are investigating a possible murder at the former Grand Hotel at 24 Elliot Street, Plymouth. That evening, the local BBC station told listeners that residents in the apartment block on the Hoe are in shock over the news, having recently learnt that the developer, Mr Charles Bartlett, may have been murdered by someone having put poison in his wine.

The following day the national media descended on the building seeking comments from residents. Most remained tight-lipped, but one source who asked not to be named expressed the view that the gruesome crime was likely to have been committed by someone who had an old grudge against Mr Bartlett, who the person claimed, had been a perfect gentleman.

A red top newspaper ran the headline, "Developer Wined, and died at Posh People's Plymouth Flats."

It was confirmed that Bartlett had been in the building with his wife two weeks prior to his recent fatal visit. Since he had most likely drunk wine then with no ill effect, it was logical to suppose the wine was tampered with in the two weeks prior to his last visit.

Meanwhile, the ire of residents was further raised when it became known that the insurance company had contacted Lynch the builder as the first port of call for compensation for the defects in the render only to find that his company had already gone into liquidation. This, unfortunately, is virtually standard practice in the industry as a means of limiting the builder's financial exposure. This new revelation meant that the Receiver, Fraser, was left with a building with completed but empty apartments and a freehold for sale. It also meant that the insurance company gobbled up the bond lodged by Bartlett with the council for £27,000 to contribute toward the cost of the demands for repairing the defects not addressed by the developer.

There was no doubt that the circumstances surrounding the Grand and the death of Bartlett were becoming murkier and murkier.

Chapter 16

But life went on.

Residents in the Grand were still understandably intrigued as to what motivation could have led to such a drastic measure being taken against Bartlett. It was assumed to be highly likely that the real motive for Bartlett's murder had nothing to do with dissatisfaction over a few cracks in the render or his rubbing salt into a few sensitive wounds by continuing to use the building as his Plymouth office. But it was a daily topic of discussion that included some unsubstantiated speculation and no little wonderment.

Curiously, there was one resident who tended to avoid engaging in dialogue about the tragic event, the quietly furtive Jeff Robins. If his Friday night ritual might seem a little odd, some might argue that so was he. Equally puzzled, Jack thought he would check out the Friday evening ritual for himself. There might be much more to Mr Robins than meets the eye.

One Friday evening he spotted Jeff heading out on his weekly adventure and wondered which restaurant was so good that he chose to eat there every week, apparently without fail. So Jack decided to do a bit of old-fashioned tailing to see if he could shed light on the mystery. Of course, it was crucial that he did this without being spotted by Jeff. He knew from his army service that discreet tailing was not easy for any lone individual to carry out, given that to do it properly would take at least four professional pursuers working as a team. So he had to stay well back in case to avoid being spotted, yet remain close enough to observe his route and not lose his quarry.

After exiting the front door of the Grand, Jeff walked purposefully down Elliot Street before crossing into Athenaeum Street, then turned right into Notte Street, past the all-night Tesco, then a sharp left into Princess Street. From there he rounded the bend into Catherine Street.

Jack had to hold back while Jeff went up the long, narrow Catherine Street, which had been named after Saint Catherine of the Catherine Wheel. In days gone by the street led directly up to the church in the Citadel, where Saint Catherine is depicted in its stained-glass windows. (Legend has it that the spiked wheel is the instrument of torture that Catherine was to suffer when she was condemned to death by the 4th century Roman Emperor Maxentius for her strong Christian beliefs. According to legend, the wheel itself broke when she touched it, so she was beheaded with a sword instead.)

Momentarily distracted by this historical nugget, Jack mused on this as he stood at the end of the narrow street while carefully keeping out of sight in case Jeff turned around. After a while he guessed it was all clear, so he strolled along, now feeling confident that Jeff was heading to the restaurant called The Treasury. Along the way, his attention was drawn to an interesting lamp overhanging a door that used to be the old police station. This was not the familiar blue lamp as seen in the vintage Z Cars television series, but the striking old Police Barracks lamp, a large impressive green object he had read about but had never seen.

After briefly admiring the ancient lamp, he resumed his mission and emerged by the door of The Treasury, which he entered on the pretext of enquiring about reserving a table in the future and requesting a copy of the menu to take away. When the waiter went to get a copy of the menu, Jack strolled around to see if he could spot Jeff, but there was no sign of him. Jack had lost him.

The following Monday, Jack drove up Catherine Street to try to discover where Jeff might have gone. He parked his car in the car park of the small Baptist church about halfway up the street. As he withdrew his ignition key, he looked up and noticed a small round window in the nondescript white gable end of a building opposite. On further inspection, he noticed that the round leaded light window showed the Jewish Star of David. Alongside the building, he noticed a short side street leading to the front entrance to the Jewish synagogue.

Abandoning his search for the night, he resolved to try again another time. Thus, to quench his curiosity, Jack joined an advertised tour of the synagogue the following week. Its curator was a veritable fountain of knowledge, not only about the synagogue itself but also regarding the development of Plymouth from a tiny village to a city over the past two-hundred-fifty years. As Jack learned, Plymouth had been a very different place back in 1762 with a tiny population. Despite its fine strategic harbour, Plymouth was not granted city status until 1928.

Jack was bemused to learn that this was because Plymouth did not have a cathedral. So he pointed out to the curator that there is a fine Roman Catholic cathedral in Plymouth in Wyndham Street, which opened in 1858. He was then told that it did not qualify since it was considered 'non-conformist'!

Bombings in the Second World War destroyed Plymouth's centre.

This gave planners the opportunity to redesign the central area as a commercial retail metropolis, and most residents living there then moved out to the suburbs. Some say this turned out to be a disaster for Plymouth and that it destroyed the beating heart of the city.

The synagogue had been established in 1762 and is believed to be the oldest Ashkenazi synagogue still in regular use in the English-speaking world. Most people, Jack included, thought that it was intentionally built in a secluded spot in a backstreet discretely away from the public eye. But its location was also chosen because of access to water. Washing of the body is a very important and mandatory requirement of Judaism, especially before meals. This requires access to clean water, which could be provided by the existing wells around Catherine Street.

Jack learnt from the curator that in order to attend a Jewish service, you must live within 2,000 cubits (equivalent to about two-thirds of an English statute mile) of the synagogue. This meant that almost all of the Jewish population of Plymouth qualified to attend the synagogue where Shabbat services were held every Friday evening at six p.m. Although there is no permanent rabbi in situ at the synagogue, a service can be held provided there are ten men in attendance.

It occurred to Jack that Jeff Robins might attend the service at the synagogue every Friday but did not want to broadcast the fact. The question was why might he want to keep it a secret, as the Jewish population in Plymouth had always enjoyed a cordial relationship with the general population. It was equally possible that he did go to dinner at The Treasury restaurant around the corner from the synagogue, as this might be more likely but this would have to be before sundown, since Sabbath is from sundown on Friday evening to sundown on Saturday evening..

Jack was aware that it was not unusual for Jewish people around the world to change their name or adjust the spelling to help them blend into the local community. Jack knew of this practice since one of his good friends in insurance was called Snyder, a mild conversion from his real Jewish name Schneider. So he asked the curator about this custom and asked for some examples of name switching. Bizarrely, one the curator volunteered, totally without prompting from Jack, was that of Robinski becoming Robins. Could it be that Jeff's family name was actually Robinski? wondered Jack.

As he left the synagogue to head back to the Grand, Jack's head was swarming with intriguing possibilities that might explain Bartlett's murder. Or might not. Either way, there were more questions to be asked and more intelligence to be gathered.

Chapter 17

Claudia Fernsby was dismissive of the police based on her experience as a magistrate and considered herself qualified to do her own investigation into the murder. She was highly suspicious of Fred Potts, whom she considered an unsuitable type for the Grand anyway. His loose talk about strangling Bartlett could just have been a cover to put people off the scent.

In her former life, Fernsby had awarded Fred a suspended sentence of twelve months and a fine of £500 for a conviction of grievous bodily harm. In effect, he had "previous".

'Haven't we met before somewhere?' she'd said to Potts.

'Yes, your worship,' he replied, 'but under different circumstances.'

She challenged him on his relationship with Bartlett and his history of GBH. Fred told her to button her lip about his GBH case since she was infringing on his human rights, and it was a diabolical liberty even mentioning it. Suitably chastised, with a swish of her wrap, Fernsby warned, 'I have my eye on you,' and walked away.

On learning that Corinne Robins had been in Plymouth the week before the discovery of Bartlett's body, DS Akesh insisted she return to Plymouth to help the police with their enquiries. She was enraged by this request but agreed to comply. At a meeting with Penhaligon and Akesh, she handed them a bound document accounting for her every moment while in Plymouth during the period when they now believed Bartlett had been murdered. She said, 'Read that first and then let me know if you have any questions.'

Penhaligon, sensing her rage, thanked her for her co-operation, and said if everyone would detail their whereabouts as comprehensively, he would be able to close the case much sooner. She then relaxed, and Penhaligon said there are just a few points he would like to clear up with her, including the time she spent with her husband during that week. This she did, and she also volunteered that she never wanted Jeff to buy the bloody apartment in the first place, but he had some fixation or other about Plymouth. The meeting ended amicably, and she gave them her contact details in case they had any further questions.

Pressure was mounting on the police to solve the case, not least because there were quite a few developers in a similar position as Bartlett with half-finished projects in administration. Might they all be at the mercy of a disappointed client out for revenge?

The media bombarded the Devon and Cornwall Constabulary for information, and occasional statements were issued by Penhaligon requesting information from the public that might help them with their enquiries. He was aware of Jack Sinnott's military and Foreign Office experiences, so he and Akesh asked him to attend a meeting at the station in Crownhill. Penhaligon did not sense that Jack was the murderer, but he was very concerned about what was revealed in interviews with other residents. It had been reported that Jack was a very nice man but had been verbally brutal when dealing with Bartlett during public meetings. Penhaligon had been told about the dispute between them over Jack having paid £25,000 for a car park lease but was prevented from opening the door of his car if a vehicle occupied the adjoining space. Bartlett had agreed he could allot him a different space, but Jack would need to pay a further £3,000 for a new space lease and the cancellation of the existing lease. Jack was furious at this and let Bartlett know his feelings in no uncertain terms.

He was somewhat taken aback when Penhaligon confronted him with this information. How on earth would he know this, wondered Jack.

Penhaligon also followed up on the fact that he was seen in the east wing of the Grand on the Thursday before Bartlett showed up. Jack was a little more forthcoming with clarification about this. He admitted that he had been in the east wing, and in addition to other issues of interest, he was keen to see exactly where Bartlett worked when in the building.

After two hours questioning, Penhaligon ended the interview and asked Jack not to leave Plymouth without informing him first. It was a strange experience for Jack to be on the other side of the desk and being questioned so rigorously rather than himself being the inquisitor. But he quite admired Penhaligon's detailed probing and the way he led Jack to admit that he did not like Bartlett and had been forceful in his dealings with the dead man.

Back in the Grand, he told Penny about the interview. She herself had already been questioned by Akesh and had told him that Jack had a run-in with Bartlett over the car park issue. But she was shocked that her Jack was being considered as a suspect.

No matter which way he looked at the situation, Jack was struggling to unearth any real clues that would direct his efforts to locate the murderer, although he was forming the view that it had to be a resident. So he decided to approach Jeff Robins quite openly and ask him if he ever visited the local synagogue. He introduced the subject by saying he had a very interesting tour of the Jewish synagogue off Catherine Street recently, describing it to Robins as a fascinating experience and a superb insight into the development of the city.

'Have you ever been there, Jeff?' he asked.

Jeff looked at him and paused, and then with a hiss and a puff and a snort just said, 'Yes, why?'

Jack said, 'I wondered if you worshipped there at their service on Fridays at six p.m.'

'What's your point?' snapped Jeff.

'Nothing really, but I couldn't help noticing you go out every Friday just before six pm and always smartly dressed, and your wife is called Corinne, which is a well-known Jewish name.'

'OK. Look, it's really none of your effing business, but if you must know, I am Jewish.'

'No problem,' said Jack. 'I just found the tour very interesting and thought that might be where you go on Fridays.'

'Do you usually go around asking people where they go at weekends?'

'It's quite intrusive, you know,' said Jeff tartly. 'I don't ask what you two do every Sunday morning in your car when you go to Wyndham Street.'

'Sorry, Jeff, I didn't mean to offend. I was just fascinated to find a synagogue in that location.'

Jack knew he was pushing his luck but thought, *It's now or never.* He asked if Jeff's family name might be Robinski, by any chance.

'What is this? A bloody interrogation or what?' snapped Jeff. 'OK. If you must know, my family name was Robinski, and it changed over a hundred years ago. What of it?'

'Nothing at all, really,' said Jack, 'only I had a friend who was Jewish, and his family did a similar thing to blend in with their environment.'

'Well guess what, maybe you should think about that,' said Jeff, 'after all, Sinnott is not exactly a well-known name around here but only in one corner of Ireland, if memory serves me right.'

'Good point, Jeff,' conceded Jack, adding a chuckle to lighten the atmosphere. 'I will give that some thought.'

Jack left the matter there and wondered if he had made any progress other than exposing a man's personal faith in a somewhat godless world. He understood Jeff's sensitivity and felt guilty for questioning Jeff the way he had. That said, Jack still felt there was something he was missing about Robins or Robinski, and in the wake of the encounter, their relationship cooled noticeably.

As the police continued to probe residents' movements in the weeks before the incident, the media kept the murder in the public mind by vaguely reporting that the Police were following a number of lines of enquiry. But they always say that, don't they?

Chapter 18

Mrs Ivy, the cleaner, was very distressed. Akesh tried to calm her by explaining that she was not under suspicion but that she might have important information about the use of keys and the details of her routine. They also wanted to speak with her assistant Molly.

The cleaning lady explained that she would visit the building at around nine a.m. on Mondays to clean apartment nineteen. Usually the apartment was empty, unless Mrs Bartlett and Mr Charles were staying overnight, which they might do some weekends. She would unlock the door, then leave the keys in the lock on the outside so that she would not lose them in the apartment and could not forget to lock up as she left.

Akesh asked to look at the key for Bartlett's office door, which he noted was a Multi-Pin Security key with the relevant security number on it. This was a standard high-security key used for all apartment entrance doors in the building. Akesh photographed it with his mobile phone for future reference and retained it as potential evidence.

To Mrs Ivy's knowledge, the only other keys to the apartment were with Mr Charles and the managing agent's office in Plymstock.

Bartlett's key was found in his pocket, confirming the assumption that he had locked the door from the inside. Akesh advised Mrs Ivy in passing that it was risky to leave the key in the door on the outside.

Mrs Ivy added she was sometimes asked to clean other apartments as a one-off when people moved in. She reeled off a few names of those who had asked her to do so, including Mrs Sinnott, Mrs Robins. 'That army marine man. I forgets his name, but his wife, Miss Charlotte, is lovely,' she said.

DS Akesh visited Molly Parks at her mother's house in Durnford Street to talk with her about her work in the Grand. She kept him on the doorstep, and even when he asked if he could come in, she refused.

She said it was her mother's house, and she hated the police, as they had put her husband away in HMP Dartmoor for ten years even though he didn't do it. She spoke with Akesh while holding her infant son balanced on her hip. She said it was terrible news about Mr Bartlett, and she was sorry for his wife, who always gave her a most welcome Christmas present of money.

Molly confirmed that she never had a key to the apartment he used and that it was always held by Mrs Ivy. Akesh asked about the identity of the baby's father, and she gave his name as Wayne Dicks, adding that her mother had thrown him out of the house as he was always getting into trouble. 'He comes to take the baby for a walk now and then. Honest facts,' she said, 'we don't really get on no more.'

'You married yourself?' she asked Akesh.

Jack was beginning to suspect that the police really had no clue as to who murdered Bartlett. But neither did he, and so he set about making his own enquiries. He thought he might start with George Fernsby, who had been very quiet of late. So he invited him for a pint one evening to get to know him a little better and see if he had any ideas.

The pair strolled down to The Dolphin on the Barbican where Jack knew the beer was always good and where they chatted for a while about how they both came to end up in Plymouth.

George explained, 'We used to live in Woking near London. It was great for commuting, but we decided to downsize from the usual five-bedroom house to an apartment in the West Country where life was a little less hectic.'

'Well, it was until recently anyway,' Fernsby added pointedly. He admitted that he was astounded at the whole affair with Bartlett and might well sell up and move from the Grand because of all the disruption the murder had caused.

Jack asked if he had known Bartlett well. George said, 'Not that well, but whenever we met, he was always pleasant and courteous. I'd have to admit that I thought he was a fine upstanding citizen who was a victim of the financial crash. You have to give the old boy credit for the conversion. A pity about the windows, though. I could have replaced all the windows with triple glazing for him, but the council insisted he retain the original windows. So much for energy efficiency. Idiots.'

He and Claudia did have some complaints about the efficiency of the thermostat on their boiler. Apparently, whenever a thermostat failed, Lynch would deal with the problem by replacing it with a working one from an empty apartment. The Fernsbys had one that had already failed. He admitted that there were a few problems like that, but nothing major, adding that their apartment, being at the rear of the building, was not affected by the damp.

George recalled that on first hearing the news, he was convinced a heart attack had killed Bartlett, or at worst, suicide, and he was shocked to be informed that he had been murdered. He said, 'Of course, old boy, you probably know Claudia is a former magistrate.'

Jack said, 'Yes, I had heard.'

'She has no confidence in the police and thinks she might have an idea of a likely suspect. I can't say anything, but you will appreciate that she has encountered all sorts of characters while on the bench, and she can smell a "bad un a mile off,"' George reckoned.

Jack asked him how he used his time in Plymouth now that he had retired from insulating the nation. 'Golf, old boy, golf,' was the reply.

'Staddon Heights is a wonderful place, marvellous people and quite a challenging course too, mind.'

Jack said the exercise must be wonderful and asked him what his handicap was. George replied, 'I was playing off eighteen but that was ten years ago. We have this new pesky Worldwide Handicap Index coming in which is confusing everyone, so I'm not sure where I stand now, old boy. But that's golf.'

'Does Claudia play?' asked Jack.

'Good Lord, no. She won't go near the place,' he said. 'Thank heavens,' he added under his breath. 'Sometimes she takes herself off for a while to her brother's farm in Cornwall for a change of air. I play every day when she's away.'

'We were last to hear the bad news as we're on the west side of the building,' explained Jack. 'Whereabouts were you and Claudia and how did you hear about it?'

'Claudia was at the a3a group book club, which she organises, and I was starting on the back nine at the golf club when I had a call from Bill Penberthy. I asked if I should return, and he said no need, as it was most likely a heart attack. So I carried on and finished the round.'

Jack was forming the view that George was a decent sort, henpecked by his wife, and was only really happy when he could see the Grand across the Sound when playing the spectacular fifth green at his favourite golf club. They strolled together back up the hill to the Grand, stopping now and then, ostensibly to admire the view, but in truth they simply needed to catch their breath.

Chapter 19

Jack was perplexed. No matter how much he racked his brain about the murder, he had to admit he was now grasping at straws. Penny even said to him, 'I don't understand why you're beating yourself up over all this. Why don't you just leave it to the police?'

In truth, his pride was hurt. He was convinced that in his previous life he would have solved the conundrum of who poisoned Bartlett in half the time. Maybe he needed a change of air and some help from old friends, he thought. He immediately recalled an old associate from his Intelligence Corps days. Trevor Downing, now retired, had also worked at GCHQ in Cheltenham and later served in MI5. Jack had not seen him since they last met at a reunion at the Hard Days Night Hotel in Liverpool where they swapped telephone numbers.

Without delay, he called Trevor and asked if he could help by checking a few names to see if there was anything about them on file.

But Trevor's immediate reply was a somewhat abrupt. 'Certainly not, old boy. Have you forgotten you signed the Official Secrets Act as have I? There's no way I can chase up people to search files for you, much as I'd love to help. Besides, you left us and went off to make your fortune in the city while we slogged our guts out for a pittance keeping you lot safe. I can't help you, mate, but would love to meet up for old time's sake. If you are ever in London, give me a hoot, and we'll break bread and down some fine grape juice.'

Jack was a bit taken aback by this response since in the old days Downing would break every rule in the book to get a result.

Initially tending to dismiss his old mate as a dead end, he decided he was not slogging it all the way to London just to wine and dine Trevor, however good a friend he might be.

So he said, 'Yes, Trevor, love to do that sometime. You take care now.'

'OK, old boy,' said Trevor. 'But before ye go, just for fun, what were the names you wanted me to look for?'

Jack gave him four names, but Trevor said he'd never heard of any of them. And then it was 'Toodle pip, old boy. Give me a shout if you decide to pop up from the country and enjoy some real civilisation. Bye.'

Bastard! thought Jack.

Penny had met Trevor when Jack was stationed in Germany and had always enjoyed his company. When Jack relayed the details of his call with him, Penny merely said, 'I keep telling you. Leave it. Let the police deal with it. Anyway, if he was that disinterested, why did he ask you for the names?'

Then a lightbulb went on in Jack's brain. 'That's it,' he said. 'Trevor's phone will still be monitored by the security services and he probably had a routine response for everyone who asked him for some inside information. Why didn't I spot that?'

He kissed Penny on the cheek and said, 'What would I do without you?'

'You'd have married some bimbo,' she said, smiling.

'So how do you fancy a bit of shopping in London? While we're up there, we can visit the girls as well,' he said to her.

To which Penny responded with an unequivocal, 'When do we leave?'

Not wanting to appear too keen, Jack thought they should leave it for a couple of weeks so they would have time to arrange to stay with their two girls and their families.

One night when Penny was away visiting her aunt in Tavistock, Jack strolled over the road and walked along Elliot Terrace Lane, crossed into Esplanade, and passed the rear entrance into the late Lady Astor's former home. He then rounded the corner into Osborne Street and entered the Conservative Club. Opting for a small corner table with a couple of chairs, he ordered a pint of mild and took a seat from where he could watch the world go by.

A constant stream of locals and visitors walked up to the Hoe to enjoy the sea view and perhaps to pay homage to the brave sailors, soldiers and airmen who fought in the two world wars and whose sacrifices were commemorated by the many memorials to the Royal Navy, Royal Air Force, the Army, the Royal Marines, the Merchant Navy and more, including those who fought in the Borneo campaign in the '60s.

After about half an hour, the Bowls Club across the road closed for the day and a few aching backs drifted into the Conservative Club. One of them was Andy Mole, who on spotting Jack, made a beeline for him.

Jack promptly offered to buy him a drink.

'Thanks, Jack. I'd love to have a pint of the amber liquid. I have a thirst you could photograph and an aching back to boot!' he said.

They sat for a good couple of hours chatting about life in general and recent events at the Grand. Jack welcomed the opportunity to hear

Andy's view on what had happened. 'Poor old Bartlett,' said Andy. 'He wasn't a bad sort really. I can't think why anyone would want to do that to him. I feel really sorry for his wife, Maddie. Lovely lady, very kind.'

He went on, 'Old Penhaligon asked me what I thought, and I told him it was very likely the murderer was someone from outside of the Grand who had something on Bartlett. The role of developer is a risky business, you know, and you need to be a bit thick-skinned to succeed and survive. If you let people down, though, they might be set on revenge, especially if they lose out financially. You know he had good contacts in the Planning Office in the Council, but one or two blokes left there for some reason, and after that Bartlett struggled to get things agreed. I'd say he upset someone along the way and he was targeted.'

Jack said, 'I reckon everyone had some issues with him, including me. How about you, Andy? How did you fare with Bartlett?'

'Good enough,' came the reply. 'We had the odd run in but nothing serious like. I'm always looking out for the new people who don't know their way around, and Lynch is not always the most helpful.'

'Didn't you have some issue over the render and the insurance cover?' queried Jack. 'I believe yours was one of those not covered because it hadn't been certified by the insurance company.'

'Yeah, too right. I did have an issue. But that wasn't really Bartlett's fault. It was his sidekick who screwed up.'

'Oh, OK, but I heard you had to cough up a big chunk of change to cover the insurance,' said Jack.

'Not too bad really, given the price I paid for the apartment. Hopefully the repairs will solve the problem. Honest facts, I'm sorry the poor bugger is gone. He added a touch of class around the place, if you know what I mean. Anyway, enough of the doom and gloom. How are you and Lady Penny settling in?'

When their glasses were empty, they strolled back to the Grand as the dark night was falling. The sodium lights on the Hoe had come on, and the navigation lights came to life in the Sound, flickering to guide sailors into the channel with sufficient draft for their crafts.

Jack retired to bed no wiser than when he got up that morning.

Chapter 20

Trevor Downing showed no surprise when Jack called to invite him to dinner at a restaurant in Devonshire Square on the edge of the Financial City. So plans were set for Jack and Penny's trip to London.

A while back, Penny had asked Charlotte if she would hold a key to number five, and also if, whenever she and Jack were away, she wouldn't mind watering the small lemon tree which thrived in the constant sun in the orangery. Penny mentioned to her that she would be in London with Jack visiting their daughters for a few days and admitted she was looking forward to a break from all the tension and suspicion in the Grand.

Overnight bags packed, Penny had also purchased a plant for her daughter Rebecca and her husband Terry and their lovely garden.

The taxi arrived on time outside the Grand front door to take them to the railway station for the train to London departing at ten-thirty a.m.

After an uneventful journey, it arrived into Paddington Station on time at two-thirty in the afternoon. They then took the underground to Waterloo, from where they took a train to Barnes, near where Rebecca lived.

On arriving at the house, they were first greeted by Rebecca's little dog Peachy, so named because of the colour of her hair, and who yapped and yapped with excitement. After a cup of tea and a biscuit

Jack took the opportunity for a siesta in case he had a late night ahead of him. This gave Penny and Rebecca a chance to chat and catch up on all their news.

Terry arrived home about five-thirty p.m., which was early for him, but he was conscious of making sure he got Jack to his appointment on time given the Friday night traffic. He was a very obliging young man who got on well with both Jack and Penny. He had recommended the restaurant because it had a private room where Jack and Trevor could talk without being overheard. The arrangement was for Jack to meet Trevor at seven p.m. sharp, and the table was reserved in the name of Sinnott.

Terry had generously offered to drive Jack there and said he would collect him after the dinner. Jack thanked him but said he would get a taxi back since it might be quite late by the time they were finished.

As Terry deftly navigated through the busy streets, they chatted idly about the murder. Arriving at his destination as planned, Jack sat by the bar to wait for Trevor, who arrived on the dot at seven p.m.

The service and the food at the chosen restaurant were excellent, and Jack allowed Trevor to select the wines which were on offer at considerable prices. They talked about everything under the sun, revisiting their times in Singapore and Borneo, and swapping stories about their various escapades. There was no mention of the four names that Jack had given Trevor, and Jack began to wonder if the dinner was a waste of time, although it was good for Penny and he to get away anyway.

Generally speaking, in meetings like this Jack felt that the English had a tendency to engage in very friendly conversation right up to the coffee when the controversial issues are dealt with. But not with Downing. At about eleven a.m. he asked the waiter to fetch their coats while Jack settled the bill with a credit card while carefully avoiding looking at the amount.

'How are you getting back to your daughter's?' asked Trevor.

Jack said, 'I thought we could stroll for a bit to the taxi rank, and I'll go from there.'

Outside the air had cooled considerably. Pulling his collar up around his neck Trevor turned to Jack and said, 'You didn't think we would discuss business in there, did you? It's all changed now since your day, my friend. Every bloody place is bugged or the waiters are wired, so you can't take any chances.'

Then moving into a somewhat conspiratorial mode, he continued, 'Listen, Jack. You can't write any of this down, and if you reveal your source, I'll have to kill you. So listen carefully.'

And then he gave Jack a generous amount of information on the four names Jack had given him.

'Robins,' Downing said, 'is like a Mad Hatter, but he's one of the brightest guys in the country. We had to get him away from London to stop the Russians getting to him. His wife is also brilliant but difficult. He's a leading expert in quantum entanglement.'

When a mystified Jack asked, 'What on earth's that?'

Downing said, 'You don't need to know, but it's pretty damn important, invaluable to the nation. Robin's father died young and his mother struggled and went into domestic service to rear him. He got a scholarship to Cambridge and received the tap on the shoulder during his graduation year. He became one of us.'

Jack's informant then went on to the subject of Bartlett. 'There's not much on Bartlett. He was a run-of-the-mill developer who did well with accommodation for students in

Devon and Cornwall. He put on airs and graces and enjoyed smooching with the upper echelons of society.'

Jack's third name had been that of Andy Mole, and Downing had lots of information on him. 'Mole is what his name suggests. It's fake. He is really Andrash Molnar from Budapest in Hungary. His father, Gorek Molnar, was an official in Budapest local government and collaborated with the Germans in sending Jewish people to the death camps. In 1944 in German-occupied Hungary, the deportation of Jews to Auschwitz began with hundreds of thousands sent to their deaths in the space of weeks. By the end of the Holocaust, some 565,000 Hungarian Jews had been murdered.

'But the Molnars escaped from Hungary to avoid being exposed for their collaboration. Mole's father came to England in 1956 after the uprising in Hungary and claimed he was a refugee fleeing from the Communists. In fact, he was a bloody spy who worked for Russia against Hungary and he continued his work in the dockyard in Plymouth. We discovered this too late and only after he died of cancer. By the time we realised it, his son Andrash was also working in the Dockyard, passing info on ship movements to the Russians via a contact he would meet at Efford Cemetery in Plymouth. He got paid when he visited Europe during his coach trips with his wife. Trained by the KGB, he knows all the tricks, but the good news is we turned him with a deal. He knew that either he co-operated or he would go down for life. He agreed, and we made sure he passed the right information to the Russians. Most of it was useless stuff any citizen could read in the Herald. But the Russians only needed one gem not in the Herald to make it worthwhile. MI5 also needed a gem every now and then to send the Russians running around like demented meerkats. We accommodated them. But

Molnar is always under pressure in case someone blows his cover and discovers he was a traitor to his own.'

Regarding Colonel de Billier, Downing described him as a typical marine who had a good innings until he screwed up an operation in Afghanistan. But he also said, 'He's loyal to the crown to a fault.

'Please mention me to him. I tried my best to help him over Afghanistan, but he was transferred into an admin job at the Citadel in Plymouth.'

With that, he spotted a vacant cab. 'I'll take this one if you don't mind. Good chatting to you, old boy. Love to Penny, and let's do it again sometime.'

As he disappeared into the dark night of London's traffic, he left Jack somewhat gobsmacked and desperately trying to remember all of the crucial information he had given him. He was actually so stunned he forgot to thank his generous informant.

But then Jack had not drunk as much wine in years.

Chapter 21

Jack arrived back at Rebecca's house after midnight. Unfortunately, all the lights were off and he didn't have a key. Peachy started barking, and a light appeared in a bedroom window.

'What time do you think this is? Where have you been? Have you been drinking?'

The entire road could here Penny Sinnott.

'We have to go, to go back,' he said to Penny.

'Go back where? We just got here!'

'I know, Penny, but we have to. You don't understand. It's not his real name.'

'Who bloody cares whether it's Robins or Robinski? Let the police deal with it.'

'No, you don't understand, love,' said Jack.

'Either you come in now and go to bed or you can sleep out there all night.'

'OK, OK. I'll explain in the morning.'

Terry, with sleep in his eyes, came down to help Jack up the stairs and guided him to the spare room where he could sleep it off on his own.

As Penny said, 'You should have left him there, silly fool. I knew he shouldn't have gone to meet that Trevor. He could never keep up with his drinking even in their army days.'

Even after a shower, two mugs of strong coffee and a bacon sandwich the following morning, Jack was still in the doghouse and hid behind his mobile, intrigued by a text message from Bill Penberthy saying, *'New development. Call me asap. Bill'.*

Jack duly phoned back and asked what was up. 'Penhaligon has had a stroke and is in Derriford Hospital. There's no suggestion of foul play.

He just buckled under the build-up of pressure from the media and his superiors. Akesh is running around desperate to make an arrest as well as a name for himself. He has already had a run-in with Fred Potts, who threatened to flatten him for his accusations. I think you need to be here, Jack.'

'OK, Bill. I'm in London now, but I'll be there mid-afternoon, assuming the railway isn't on strike again.'

Penny said, 'So that's it then, is it? What about Jennie, who has taken the day off specially to meet up with us and go shopping?'

'Sorry, love. You stay and meet with Jennie and give her my love. I just have to get back, or there will be a terrible miscarriage of justice.'

'Off you go again. It's been the same all through our marriage, there one minute and gone the next,' complained Penny.

'Sorry. I need to check train times to Plymouth from Paddington.'

Then to his daughter, 'Rebecca, how do I get from here to Paddington?'

Fuming with rage at Jack's disruption of their plans, Penny was banging dishes in the kitchen. 'Bloody Irishmen,' she muttered. 'You just can't rely on them for anything.'

Jack used his senior rail card to avail of the discount for a first-class ticket on the Great Western leaving Paddington at eleven-fifteen a.m. and arriving Plymouth 15.10. He bought a newspaper and a bar of chocolate at the kiosk, his head still throbbing from the night before.

It was mid-term school break, the West Country beckoned, and the station was heaving with mums and school-children.

After he paid for the paper and chocolate, he turned around to find two policemen standing behind him, one a sergeant and the other a rookie with a photograph in his hand and who asked if he was Mr Jack Sinnott.

In amazement he smiled and said, 'As a matter of fact I am.' Then they asked where he was going, and he said, 'Plymouth. Why?'

'Can we see your ticket, please, sir?' one asked.

'Sure,' said Jack, handing them the ticket he had just purchased.

'Can you step over here, please, for a moment. We need to ask you some questions,' said the sergeant.

'Wait a minute,' said Jack. 'This is some sort of "candid caught on camera" joke, right?'

Offended by the suggestion, the Sergeant said, 'No, sir. It's no joke. There's a warrant out for your arrest.'

'What?' said Jack. 'What on earth for?'

'We have been informed that you were instructed not to leave Plymouth without first informing Chief Inspector Penhaligon.'

Jack smacked his forehead with his hand, saying, 'Oh no! You're right. You are absolutely so right. I did agree to let him know, but I'm returning there now. I completely forgot. It's been a bit hectic of late.'

'DS Akesh in Plymouth needs to speak with you urgently,' said the sergeant.

'OK,' said Jack guiltily, 'but can you get him on the phone now and see if we can sort this out and save you the trouble of the paperwork?

'One of the reasons I'm rushing back to Plymouth is to assist DS Akesh with his enquiries into a murder. I would like to speak with him to explain.'

After a couple of calls, they successfully got hold of Akesh. Jack apologised and told him he would be arriving on the 15.10 into Plymouth. The sergeant then spoke with Akesh, and they agreed to let Jack go, although they hung around long enough to make sure he actually boarded the train.

Relieved, Jack settled into his first-class seat with a table between the two rows. A mum and three children under seven shared the seats on either side of the table. The children were comparatively well-behaved for the first three hours of the journey before a typical restlessness began to appear. Much to Jack's discomfort, a gradually-escalating racket had nearly ended in World War III by the time the train slowed and glided along the edge of the river Plym on its way into Plymouth Railway Station.

On alighting, Jack immediately headed for the taxi rank where a pleasant Chinese man said, 'Ooh the Grand, very bad murder there.'

'Really,' said Jack. 'I hadn't heard. Been away, you know.'

Jack called DS Akesh to confirm he had arrived and was heading up to the Grand to freshen up but would be available if he needed to contact him. He then called Bill Penberthy and said he needed time to shower and to grab something to eat, so they agreed to meet in The Gladstone Room at five-thirty p.m. where both had news to share.

And the news was not inconsiderable.

According to Penberthy, Chief Inspector Penhaligon's stroke meant he was not expected to return to work for at least six weeks. Even more intriguing, Akesh has been grilling Jeff Robins about his mother, Esther Robins, who, it was now revealed, was actually the unpopular and mysterious head housekeeper in the Grand on the morning of the fire. Her husband had died young, leaving her with no money and one child to care for. That child was none other than our Jeff Robinski, aka Robins. Apparently, she always took Fridays off, worked weekends and was another regular at the Plymouth Synagogue in Catherine Street.

Bill said that Akesh was now following a line of inquiry based on his suspicion that Jeff had a grudge against Bartlett because he had blamed his mother for starting the fire. He was also wondering why the family had changed their name.

Jack asked about Jeff's whereabouts. Bill said, 'That's the problem, Jack. He's gone. No one knows where. He just vanished.'

Chapter 22

Police had promptly sent out an urgent bulletin and a photograph to seaports and airports in their efforts to track down the mysteriously-vanished Jeff Robins. When his wife was asked to return to Plymouth, she refused. However, Jack was quite relaxed about Jeff's disappearance and had a good idea of where he might be. He also decided to reveal nothing of the information he had acquired about Andy Mole for now.

That night Jack called Trevor Downing. It was an odd situation. Jack asked if he got home all right last evening. Trevor said, 'What do want, Jack? You know the rules.'

'Nothing like that, old boy,' Jack said. 'I just wanted to thank you for the other evening; it was most enjoyable. But here's a hypothetical question for you. A forty-year-old man critical to the security of the nation is accused of something he didn't do and decides to disappear. Where do you think he might go?'

'What sort of question is that? You writing a book or something?'

'Something like that,' Jack said.

'No idea, old boy. Can't help you with that one. Oh, by the way, I forgot to mention last night that I've had a whole new alarm system fitted in the cottage. It makes it a really safe house now.'

'Thanks, Trevor, sorry to bother you.'

Jack smiled as he switched off his mobile, thinking, 'That's it; I suspected as much. They've got him tucked away in a safe house.'

He then called Penny at Jennie's house to apologise for last evening.

As ever, she understood but had worried if he'd got home OK and had enough to eat. 'Jennie and I had a lovely day's shopping,' she added. 'We had lunch at Claridge's too. It's so nice there.'

Her husband explained the situation in Plymouth. 'Things are moving very fast here, love, but I think it'll all be sorted by tomorrow. Tell you what, why don't I get the train to London the day after tomorrow, and we can go to a ballet or something.'

'Don't be daft,' she said. 'Have you any idea what that would cost?'

Jack said, 'To hell with the cost. You're worth it.'

'Oh, give over with the *plámás,*' said Penny. 'Anyway, I'll call you tomorrow evening, and we can decide then.'

Somehow the Herald newspaper had got wind of Jeff Robins' disappearance and made it headline news. 'A source in the Grand informed our reporter that a Dr Jeffrey Robins, who is employed at Devonport Dockyard and sometimes lectures at Plymouth University, is wanted by the police to help with their inquiries into the recent murder of the well-known developer Mr Charles Bartlett at the Grand in Plymouth.'

The next day, DS Akesh called everyone to the Gladstone Room at six p.m. with a view to learning more about Robins and finding out who knew about his mother's work situation.

As the residents gradually began arriving for the meeting, you could feel a sense of excitement mixed with eager anticipation. Doctor Phil Hoskin altered his shift in order to attend. Fred Potts looked ready to take on all comers as he sat in the middle of the large powder-blue sofa. Bill and Louise sat with Jack. Colonel de Billier Fortescue and Charlotte brought along Jessie who sniffed everyone and then sat patiently with one paw on Fortescue's right foot. Claudia Fernsby and George sat front of house, she looking as if she felt entitled to be behind the table holding court. Andy Mole limped in complaining about his hip but otherwise looking relaxed. He then proceeded to work the room, reassuring everyone that it would all be over just as soon as they find Robins. Personally, he said he liked old Jeff even though he was a very odd man, acknowledging it was a very difficult time for his wife, Corinne, too, of course.

Sergeant Akesh thanked everyone for coming at this difficult time. He introduced Inspector Dolmore from the constabulary who had been assigned to the case at very short notice and who admitted he was playing catch-up. Akesh asked Dr Hoskin to give a brief update on the health of Penhaligon who had won the respect of all in the Grand. He then proceeded to outline recent events and stated that the police urgently needed to talk with Dr Jeff Robins in connection with the murder of Mr Bartlett. He also briefly touched on the fact that Esther Robins was Jeff's mother.

Akesh was clearly in full-on bloodhound mode and eager to nab Robins. The fact that the latter had disappeared convinced him of his guilt. Most of the residents who already held the view that Robins was a very odd man now reckoned he was most likely guilty.

Although this brought a sense of shock to the meeting, there was also a feeling of relief that the tragic affair might be coming to an end at last.

Since it was common knowledge that there had been bad blood between Bartlett and Robins for obvious reasons, Akesh asked if anyone in the room had any information about Robins or if they were aware of Robins' family history. Claudia Fernsby suggested he might have gone to Scotland to be with his wife, Corinne.

Andy Mole believed he would have already skipped the country and could be anywhere. 'Didn't he work on secret weapons or something in the Dockyard?' he asked. 'He could be in Russia by now,' he mused, and some people laughed at the suggestion.

Jack Sinnott asked if the police had ruled out all other lines of inquiry.

Before Akesh could respond, Inspector Dolmore cut in to say, 'Certainly not. We still have to keep an open mind, but we do need to talk with Mr Robins as soon as possible.'

Jack pressed them further, suggesting that Jeff's supposed motive did not sound particularly plausible. Dolmore replied, saying, 'Yes, coming to this case with fresh eyes is both an advantage and a disadvantage, but we still must keep an open mind.'

Jack noticed Andy Mole shifting uneasily in his chair. Jack said, 'It is still possible that the guilty party might be in this very room right now.'

'How come?' quizzed Mole.

'In life I've found nothing is ever quite what it seems on the surface,' said Jack.

'For example,' challenged Mole.

'Well, just as an example, Andy, Mole is not your real name. Am I right?'

It was like an Exocet missile had just shattered the Grand. Everyone turned, stared at Andy and waited for his response as he went red in the face. Akesh started to speak, but Dolmore stopped him.

Mole then said, 'It certainly is my name, and I have the papers to prove it.'

Jack said, 'I'm sure you have, Andy, but it wasn't always your name, was it?'

'OK. So what was it then?' said Mole.

'How about Andrash Molnar for starters?' said Jack.

'Oh that,' said Andy. 'Why didn't you say so first? God, you Irish do make things complicated, making mountains out of molehills.' He looked around the room for support and not noticing his unintended pun on his name. 'My parents were called Molnar years ago, and they changed the family name to Mole. It's not a crime, you know.'

'Sure, but you also said they were from Cornwall.'

'What of it?' demanded Mole.

'Molnar is not a very Cornish name, is it?'

Mole shrugged his shoulders and said, 'I was very young then, but I was brought up in Cornwall.'

'That's fine, Andy, but why lie about it? Your parents didn't come from Cornwall at all. They came from Hungary, didn't they?'

Jack could see he had clearly touched a nerve. 'What if they did? That's not a crime either. Anyway, what has all this got to do with the reason we're here tonight?'

Despite his dismissals of Jack's questions, Andy was beginning to show signs of stress as beads of sweat slowly made their way down his cheeks. Some residents even felt sorry for him, but Jack had definitely rattled his cage.

Sgt Akesh said, 'Mr Sinnott, what are you getting at? We haven't got all night here.'

'Well, Sergeant,' explained Jack. 'I was just trying to point out that things are never quite what they seem on the surface, hence a real need to keep an open mind.'

Charlotte raised her hand and asked DS Akesh if it might be possible to have a short break, pointing out that she had the equipment to prepare coffee or tea for everyone. 'An excellent idea,' said Inspector Dolmore quickly, before his bloodhound Akesh could throw cold water on the suggestion.

As the mood in the room had become rather tense, it actually made for a welcome break.

Chapter 23

Bill said quietly to Jack, 'How long have you known all this about Andy?'

'Just found out recently, Bill,' said Jack.

Inspector Dolmore approached Jack and asked if he was withholding information that could be helpful in their investigation. Jack said, 'I'm not sure yet, but I don't believe that Jeff Robins is guilty of murdering Bartlett.'

'Why so sure?'

'Well, the motive is weak. I mean, you don't usually murder someone just because he cast a slur on your mother.'

'OK, so who do you think is guilty?'

'I'm not sure yet, but we might find out tonight.'

The meeting resumed when Akesh said, 'OK, let's get on with it.'

Mole asked if he could say something with regard to Mr Sinnott's comments. 'Inspector, Sergeant Akesh, I would like to make a formal complaint about the comments made by Mr Sinnott in revealing my original family name. I consider this to be a gross infringement of my human rights and the new personal data protection regulations.'

The inspector simply said, 'Noted. But we need to get back to the subject at hand.'

Then Jack said, 'Can we just put the record straight here? Mr Mole had just as much reason as any one of us to murder Bartlett. In fact, he had more in many ways, as he was financially disadvantaged over the insurance. He was also overheard having a blazing row with Bartlett in the car park. He had the opportunity to copy the key to apartment nineteen given that it was in the door while Mrs Ivy was cleaning it and it's right across the landing from his own apartment number twenty.'

'Utter nonsense,' said Mole, 'just because a key is in the door doesn't mean you can copy it. These are secure keys and very difficult to copy.'

'Indeed,' said Jack, 'but you and I know, Andy, that to copy a key, all you need is a mobile phone and a small ruler for scale.' Mole's face went puce as Jack continued. 'You photograph the key and the ruler to give you scale, and the rest, as you know, is easy.'

Mole now realised that Jack knew he was a spy, but Jack was sworn to secrecy and could not reveal the whole story.

'Well, anyone can look that up on YouTube. It's common knowledge,' said Mole.

From their murmurings, it was clear that most people in the room had never heard of this key-copying technique.

'Anyway,' said Mole, 'are you accusing me of murdering Bartlett?'

'No,' said Jack. 'I'm just pointing out the theoretical possibility. While everyone seems to be convinced that it was Jeff Robins it could be someone else in this room or outside it.'

'So exactly what motive could I possibly have for killing Bartlett? This is getting ridiculous, Inspector,' said Mole.

Now Jack was in a dilemma. He could not reveal all he knew, so he thought he would fly a few kites to see where they might land. 'Well, as you said to me yourself the other night in the club, Bartlett might have something on someone; he might know something about their past and had threatened to use it if they did not cooperate with one of his schemes. He might know something about you and your family, for example, that you did not want disclosed to residents in the Grand.'

More beads of sweat began to appear on Mole's forehead. Akesh was getting increasingly uneasy with this discussion, convinced as he was that the real murderer had already absconded. But Dolmore sensed that Jack knew more than he was revealing and wanted the tussle between him and Mole to continue.

Mole continued to protest, saying, 'I have nothing to hide. My life is an open book.'

Jack said, 'So you say, but we didn't know you were from Hungary, which I think is interesting. Tell us more. When did your family leave Hungary and why?'

'The uprising in 1956,' said Mole, 'We fled as refugees to get away from the Russians.'

'Oh really, and what did your late Dad do in Hungary, Andy?'

'That's actually none of your business. You Irish flooded the UK with your navvies around the same time.'

'Well, to be fair now, Andy, the UK needed workers in '56 to help them rebuild houses and roads after the war, and by the way, the word navvies comes from workers building harbours and breakwaters for the safe navigation of British shipping. You mentioned that your dad worked in the dockyard and you followed in his footsteps.'

'That's right. We refugees contributed to this country as well as you Irish, you know.'

'I'm sure you did, and good on you for that, but as we've already established, nothing is ever quite what it seems, Andy, and some people used their work in military establishments as cover for their real mission.'

'Which is?' asked Andy.

'Well, it can be to learn a new skill to use later back in their own country like the Japanese did, or to transfer secret technology to another nation. It might even be to spy on this country for a foreign power, that sort of thing.'

At this point, Andy went silent. Everyone looked at his bowed head.

Then lifting his head, he looked straight at Dolmore and said, 'Inspector, I need to speak with you in private, please.'

Dolmore said, 'OK, ladies and gentlemen, thank you for coming this evening; you have been most helpful. Mr Mole, I would like you to remain in the room.'

Akesh was now furious with Dolmore, who seemed to have taken control of Akesh's investigation.

The other residents went about returning to their respective apartments, and Bill and Louise walked up the stairs with Jack.

'What on earth was that all about, Jack?' said Bill.

'Well, Bill, life is never…'

'I know,' said Bill, 'life is never quite what it seems.'

'Let's see what happens tomorrow. I'm drained,' said Jack.

And Bill looked at him, now deeply suspicious that Jack knew more than he was admitting.

The following morning, residents were shocked to learn that Jeff Robins was seen jogging on the Hoe as cool as could be. He claimed he had popped up to Scotland to see Corrine and decided to stay for a few days.

On the other hand, Andy Mole was no longer in the Grand. He had been taken to Crownhill Police Station, where he said he would make a statement on the understanding that his past would not be made public. He asked for a guarantee of anonymity about his past, or else he would reveal that he had helped to protect the UK in its counter-espionage against Russia.

Dolmore said that he would have to refer the matter up the line and would come back to him. Mole declined the offer of a solicitor.

Meanwhile, he was being detained on suspicion of involvement in the death of Bartlett.

The following day, instructions were sent from the Home Office directly to the Chief Constable of the Devon and Cornwall Constabulary. Mole was to be given an assurance that his past activities would not be disclosed, but he is to be charged with premeditated murder based on his statement and further investigations. Mole's detailed statement outlined how he had managed the murder and claimed he had been driven to protect the residents of the Grand who were like family to him.

A statement was subsequently issued by the Chief Constable to the media, but he declined to take any questions.

Residents were further shocked when they heard this news and many still felt sorry for the lovely, helpful old man Andy Mole.

On the train to Paddington the following day Jack bought himself a small screwcap bottle of red wine but idly checked that there were no holes in the cap. Relaxed by the wine and the motion of the train, he reflected on his life and family.

Jack and Penny's two daughters had by now attended university.

Jennie had qualified in nursing at Hammersmith Hospital and Rebecca qualified as a printed textile designer, and went on to read for her Masters at the famous Central St. Martins in London. They had both married and had children, all girls except "the prince", as Penny referred to Oscar, the only grandson who, like his grandfather was brilliant on the running track, as well as having film-star looks. Both daughters lived on the outskirts of London and loved to visit Plymouth for a change of air and some fishing.

Lost in his family reverie, Jack dozed off in the empty first-class compartment, waking up as they passed the Old Heinz factory in Harlesden. He had advised Penny, 'Expect me when you see me.'

At Paddington he jumped into a black cab and asked the driver to take him to Barnes. The cab driver was a chatty soul and said, 'You OK there, gov?'

Jack said, 'Yes, fine. Thank you.'

'Retired now, are ye?' the cabbie asked.

'Yes,' said Jack. 'As a matter of fact, I have been for six years now.'

'Boring, I bet. Is it?'

'Sometimes,' said Jack.

'Well, I always say you never know what might happen. Life is never quite what it seems. It can even be full of surprises, you know. Take the other day. I picks up an old bloke and asks him what he done like when he was working, and you know, what he said? He said he was a major in the Intelligence Corps in the army, worked at GCHQ, you know the doughnut building in Cheltenham, and then joined MI5. I said, yeah, pull the other one, mate.'

Then he said, 'Well, if I told you what I really did, you would never believe me. Funny old bloke he was.'

Penny and Rebecca were pleased to see Jack and to catch up on his hot news about the investigation and the progress the police were making.

When Penny said, 'Aren't our police wonderful really?' Jack said nothing.

After a restful night and a hearty full Irish breakfast, he and Penny made their way to their other daughter Jennie's home to spend some quality time with her and her family.

Maybe life was about to return to normal.

Chapter 24

Back in Plymouth, after a series of probing interviews with the police, Mole was arrested and formerly charged with the murder of Charles Bartlett.

A week later, at a preliminary hearing held "in camera" at Plymouth Crown Court at 10 Armada Way, Mole was asked by the judge how did he plead to the charge, and he replied, 'Not guilty, your honour.'

The judge recorded the plea and said that a date would now be set for a full hearing at Bristol Crown Court and that the proceedings would be again held in camera. In Camera proceedings mean that the Competent Authority/Court allows only those persons who are essential to the proceedings to be present while hearing and deciding the witness protection application or deposing in the court. The date for the hearing was set for March 17, a special date for Jack.

At the Grand, there was some relief that the saga was finally heading towards a satisfactory conclusion while there was some sympathy and sadness all round for both Bartlett and Mole. Interestingly, there were no more leaks to the press, and residents agreed that it would be inappropriate to comment on the murder to anyone.

Ahead of the hearing, Jack arranged to meet with Jeff Robins for dinner at the Treasury restaurant one Saturday evening after sundown in an attempt to make amends and rebuild their former good relationship. Jeff invited Jack to join him at the synagogue for the service in advance of the meal, which Jack agreed to on condition, that Jeff would attend an Easter service at the Cathedral in Wyndham Street. They became good friends over subsequent months and remained so for years.

The Crown Court jury in Bristol was sworn in and consisted of seven men and five women. The trial was heard by Judge Mr Sessions-Hodge. In addition to police and coroner's evidence, Madeline Bartlett and Jack Sinnott were also called to give evidence at the proceedings. This was an ironic way for Jack to be spending Saint Patrick's Day when he would normally be partying.

In truth, this was a murder trial with a twist, in that Mole was technically still an agent of the British government. At the hearing, the prosecuting barrister, Ms Wherry, asked Mole why he had pleaded not guilty, having already signed a statement at a police interview clearly stating that he had injected poison into the wine with the intention of murdering Bartlett.

Mole claimed that he had been put under great pressure by Mr Sinnott at a gathering in the Gladstone Room in the Grand due to the many insinuating assertions before he was interviewed by the police.

He pointed out that he had done great work for the British Government, and he was not well due to his aching hip and was still grieving for his late wife, Alice. When challenged, he admitted that he had also been under pressure because of Bartlett but said he only wanted to frighten him by putting a little of the poison in his wine.

He claimed that he never intended to murder him and was astonished and extremely sorry when he was declared dead.

Jack was then called to the stand and asked to take the judicial oath by swearing on the Bible to tell the truth, the whole truth, etc., but he refused, prompting gasps of surprise around the courtroom.

The judge said, 'Did you say you refuse to swear under oath, Mr Sinnott?'

'Yes, your honour,' said Jack.

'Why ever not?' asked the judge.

'Well, your honour, as a Roman Catholic, I object to a judicial swearing on oath, but I am happy to provide an affirmation instead.' (An affirmation is a verbal, solemn and formal declaration made in place of an oath while having the same effect as an oath.)

'I understand,' said the judge, and he then ordered the Clerk of the Court to provide Jack with the wording for the affirmation which Jack duly read as follows: 'I solemnly and sincerely declare and affirm that the evidence I shall give will be the truth, the whole truth and nothing but the truth.'

Jack was then challenged by the defending barrister, Mr Kant, a seasoned middle-aged man well known to the judge. He asked Jack why he pressured Mr Mole at the gathering in the Gladstone Room in the Grand and also asked if Jack was privy to some secret information which he should have shared with the police.

Jack replied that he was not privy to any special information.

'So,' the barrister then said. 'You obviously suspected Mr Mole of some wrongdoing.' Jack acknowledged that he was curious and sceptical about Mr Mole.

'So, what exactly made you suspect him?' asked Mr Kant.

Quick as a flash Jack answered, 'A chance remark.'

'Which was?' queried Kant.

'Fenekig,' replied Jack.

'Which means what exactly, Mr Sinnott?' asked the barrister.

'Well, sir,' said Jack. 'It's a Hungarian greeting like "cheers or nostrovia".'

'So what?' said the barrister.

'Mr Mole used it at a barbecue, and when asked to explain it, he said it was a greeting used in the Czech Republic.'

'And your point is, Mr Sinnott?' intervened the judge.

'Well, your honour, Mr Mole knew quite well that this is a Hungarian greeting, so why claim it to be from the Check Republic?'

The barrister then asked how Jack knew about Mole's name change, and Jack replied that there is an abundance of information available in records, which he researched, and the police and the general public have access to the same records.

'No more questions,' said the defending barrister.

The prosecuting barrister, Ms Wherry, asked for Mrs Bartlett to be called to the stand. After her swearing in, the barrister offered her condolences and said she would try to be brief given the distressing circumstances surrounding her husband's untimely death. After a few preliminary questions, she honed in on Mole's relationship with Bartlett. Madeline Bartlett claimed they did have some heated arguments but was not aware of all the details.

'Can you remember any remarks made by your late husband in relation to Mr Mole?' she was asked.

'Well,' she replied, 'I recall that Mr Mole was very angry over the insurance mix-up, but he backed off when Charles told him he knew he was from Hungary and if he was smart, he would just pay up and shut up. I'm not sure what the Hungary thing was all about.'

After a few more questions, Mrs Bartlett was stood down from the witness box in tears.

In all, the hearing took two days and by mid-afternoon on the second day the jury were sent out to consider their verdict. They returned after an hour with a unanimous verdict of "guilty of premeditated murder in the first degree". Mole/Molnar was sentenced to twenty years, to be served in a prison in the north of England.

In a formal sense it ended there, but, as it's often the case in these matters, it didn't quite fade as a topic of conversation in some quarters.

Inevitably, rumours circulated about why the case had been heard in a closed court, and it did not take much for some to work out that Jack Sinnott knew much more than he had let on.

Chief Inspector Penhaligon recovered well from his stroke, which turned out to be more of a warning than a real stroke. He went on to enjoy his retirement surrounded by his family.

When the following Christmas came around, a package was delivered to Trevor Downing's home in London containing six bottles of fine red wine, but no note, no card and no indication of who had sent it.